THE AMUSING LIFE

SONG SOKZE

THE AMUSING LIFE
A COLLECTION OF STORIES

TRANSLATED BY SE-UN KIM

DALKEY ARCHIVE PRESS

Originally published in Korean as Jaeminaneun Insaeng by Kang Publishing Ltd. in 1997.
Copyright © 1997 by Song Sokze
Translation copyright © 2016 by Se-un Kim

First Dalkey Archive edition, 2016

Library of Congress Cataloging-in-Publication Data
Identifiers: ISBN 9781628971798
LC record available at https://catalog.loc.gov/

Partially funded by a grant by the Illinois Arts Council, a state agency
Published in collaboration with the Literature Translation Institute of Korea

Dalkey Archive Press publications are, in part, made possible through the support of the University of Houston-Victoria and its programs in creative writing, publishing, and translation.

Dalkey Archive Press
Victoria, TX / McLean, IL / Dublin
www.dalkeyarchive.com

Cover design and composition by Mikhail Iliatov
Printed on permanent/durable acid-free paper

Foreword to the Revised Edition

WHEN I PUBLISHED this book in 1997, I didn't consider that books have lives of their own and that life can always transform into a different type of life. It doesn't stop there. The life of the person who writes the book can also transform into a different type of life. Thinking brought with it transformation and things continue to transform.

Right from the start, I never wanted to comment on the form or appearance of novels. One thing I do want to mention, however, is that the genre of the novel tolerates so much, and that's the reason why someone like me has been able to wander within it. When you think about it, they're all that way—literature, life, etc. Whatever I set out to try, it would open its vast arms and welcome me in. The first edition of *The Amusing Life* was a product of generous toleration.

In this revised edition, I've added the "story" from Mandarin Fish (May, 1998), which was published after *The Amusing Life*, and have also taken out or condensed material which seemed overly dependent on the genre's toleration (of course, according to my current judgment). It's possible that the things that once left will come back, and the things that are present will move out. If something I didn't realize then or forgot about wants to come in, it just might come in. It's my opinion that nothing is conclusive in a novel. If you ask me to find something that's unchanging, it's the fact that all of the universe, its spirit and mold, keeps changing.

Perhaps a revised edition will bear another revised edition. Maybe a change in the edition, the title, the author, or nothing at all. Isn't that what will make this an amusing life?

—In the late spring of 2004, Song Sokze

TABLE OF CONTENTS

NUMBER

THE BASIC TRAINING of soldier number 9 of the ROK Army's 7th Division, 26th Regiment, 3rd Battalion, 2nd Company, 1st Platoon, 3rd Squad was disrupted by soldier number 8. Soldier number 8 of the ROK Army's 7th Division, 26th Regiment, 3rd Battalion, 2nd Company, 1st Platoon, 3rd Squad was a harmless fellow from a remote village near the ROK Army's 7th Division, 26th Regiment, 3rd Battalion who knew little about the world except for farming.

In the army, they use numbers to keep track of soldiers, to instill a sense of belonging, and to keep minds alert. In other words, when soldiers are lined up and the drill sergeant stands to the side and shouts, "Head count!" Number 1 shouts "one," Number 2 shouts "two," Number 3 shouts "three," and so on. However, soldier number 8 of the ROK Army's 7th Division, 26th Regiment, 3rd Battalion, 2nd Company, 1st Platoon, 3rd Squad, whose world consisted of farming and not much else and whose farthest journey from home was the thirty-nine kilometers from his house to the guard post of the ROK Army's 7th Division, 26th Regiment, 3rd Battalion, used his own unique intonation and vocabulary to state his number. There was no other way number 8 could say it. When it was his turn, number 8 shouted, "Ya-ight." When this happened, number 9 momentarily forgot where he was and laughed out loud.

The drill instructor in charge of the basic training of the ROK Army's 7th Division, 26th Regiment, 3rd Battalion, 2nd Company decided that if there was someone laughing during line up in the rigorous army, neither rigor nor the army could be properly maintained. Accordingly, the instructor kicked number 9 in the shins.

Soldier number 9 of the ROK Army's 7th Division, 26th Regiment, 3rd Battalion, 2nd Company, 1st Platoon, 3rd Squad didn't mean to laugh, but he couldn't help the outburst. After being kicked in the shins, he reminded himself that he shouldn't make the stupid mistake of laughing out loud during line up in the rigorous army. He only had two shins after all. And even if he had hundreds of shins, all of them would hurt if they were kicked.

"Head count, again!"

"Wu-uhn!"

Number 9 didn't laugh.

"To-woo!"

That wasn't funny.

"Thu-ree!"

Laughing didn't even occur to him.

"Fo-or!"

His shins were still sore.

"Fi-eve!"

That was when it felt like something as light as foam crept up his waist.

"Si-ix!"

Something seemed to bite the soles of soldier number 9.

"Se-ven!"

Number 9 bit his lip and clenched his fists. Laughing meant death. But—

"Ya-ight."

That voice, so annoyingly small. Number 9 once again had forgotten that he was number 9 and broke out in laughter. The drill sergeant ran over in a huff.

"Are you kidding me?"

Number 9 was ready to cry.

"No, sir!"

"You think I'm an idiot?"

He wanted to cry, number 9.

"No, sir!"

"Then why would you laugh?"

The drill sergeant seemed like a person of reason. But merciless were his combat boots and fist.

"If this kind of shit happens again, all of you will circle the training ground crawling with your heads on the ground and arms behind your backs. Be sure of that. Head count, again!"

He tried not to laugh, that number 9. But that made it worse. All of the trainees of the ROK Army's 7th Division, 26th Regiment, 3rd Battalion, 2nd Company loathed number 9. Even number 8 grumbled at him. But that only made it worse for number 9. Later on, not the "Ya-ight" but the mere sight of number 8's butt rounding the training field, forehead to the ground was enough to set him off. The eyes of a breathless number 8, which were emerging from his crotch, shot a blameful look at number 9, and even that made him laugh. Watching the drill sergeant getting angry also made him burst out (in laughter). Tears rolling down his cheeks, sweating, and clutching his shins, he just couldn't not laugh. Soldier number 9 of the ROK Army's 7th Division, 26th Regiment, 3rd Battalion, 2nd Company, 1st Platoon, 3rd Squad was the first soldier to replace the word "nine" with the sound of laughter.

SWIM CLASS

AS THE DAYS got warmer, and the clothes became lighter, his wife's nagging took on a tone of genuine worry.

"My goodness, look at that stomach."

"You've seen it forever. What's wrong with my belly?"

He nonchalantly stuck out his belly. But the truth was that he was feeling some discomfort because it felt like a pumpkin had attached itself to his stomach over the winter.

"I just don't get it. Do you have another wife I don't know about? How can you be gaining weight when I don't give you anything to eat?"

His wife tilted her head questioningly. The reason for the weight gain was simple. The problem was that he didn't like to move. It wasn't like that in his younger days, when he'd first started his business. He worked actively and tended to the job more physically. Exercise was taken care of. But once his business got settled with more employees, the younger people did most of the work and he didn't have to move around as much. Take driving as an example. He started to drive more frequently. He'd take his car even to the corner shop just one or two hundred meters away. Even if it felt like he wasn't eating much, the small helpings of food consumed, alongside alcohol, while entertaining clients or during get-togethers with people at the office added up. Most of it was high in protein and fat, so it meant that he was eating far more calories than the calories in the regular meals he'd have consumed at home.

"We have to do something about this. Honey, you should go hiking in the nearby hills at sunrise or something."

"Who has time at sunrise?"

"Just get up a little bit earlier."

"When I wake up at dawn, how should I put this, other things come to mind. Rather than groaning my way up a hill, we should do productive and efficient things that are more inter-personal, you know?"

His wife, who was five years younger than him, glanced upwards with her youthful, pretty eyes, which still reminded him of the days when they'd dated.

"Dear, you must think I'm joking. No. I'm taking action."

The next day, without delay, his wife headed to the nearby health club and signed him up for swim classes. That evening after dinner, there was more bickering.

"Why swimming of all sports? There are so many other sports out there."

"Just think of it as bathing every morning."

His wife continued to explain that there was no better sport than swimming for losing weight, and unlike hiking or soc-cer clubs, one could swim rain or shine. The health club was a pretty well-known one, with some big shot politicians from both political parties holding memberships in the past. Being so well-known, it was expensive as well. However, that wasn't the prob-lem. The membership card for the class his wife had signed him up for indicated that classes were from five to six every morning, with three days of lessons and three days of free swimming, and next to it were written the words, "Beginner's Class."

"I tell you, I swam across the Han River and back in my younger days. But this is what you sign me up for? This class is for people who swim like bricks."

"Oh, I had no idea. I thought the only part of you that'd float would be your mouth, the way you talk so much."

He wasn't exaggerating. His doggy paddle was indeed as good as the next guy's in his younger days.

"You can go if you want. I'm not going to a beginner's class even if I die drowning."

"Just go. You can go and change classes."

The next morning he headed to the health club, grumbling. The club employee was very thin, almost painfully skinny.

"Oh, no. The other classes are full for this month."

In that case, he said, he wanted his money back. The employee looked over his body and facial expression, giving him a funny look before she carefully continued talking.

"Since you've already signed up, why don't you try the beginner's class just once? The class is in session. Try it today, and if you don't like it we'll give you your money back."

When he replied saying that he hadn't brought his swimsuit, she quickly offered to lend him one. He grumbled again as he changed into it. He grumbled once more when he felt the squeeze of the swimsuit on his lower belly as he headed to the pool.

Once he entered the pool zone he couldn't believe his eyes. Dozens of beautiful women were paddling with nothing but their swimsuits on. Of course, there was nothing strange about wearing a swimsuit in a swimming pool. But he was already exclaiming, "Holy smokes!" before he could stop himself. To hide his embarrassment, he asked the employee who walked behind him, "Are all of the students young ladies?"

"No. The morning class is mostly people with day jobs. It's just that this month we didn't have any men sign up."

Before too long, he caught sight of a slim beauty who reminded him of his wife before they married. She was the instructor and was explaining basic swimming methods to the students, water dripping from her hair. He quietly sneaked himself in among the students. The moment the instructor noticed him, she blinked her eyes, as if surprised. That too gave his heart a tremble. He silently cried, "Viva! Long live Korea!" although he couldn't figure out why those words came to mind.

"OK, we're going to practice what we learned. Everybody into the water."

After finishing her explanation, she herself was the first to enter the water, and in great form. He stopped himself just before diving into the water like the instructor. It occurred to him that since he was enrolled in the beginner's class, he should in fact act like a beginning swimmer. He couldn't let them find out the truth and advance him to the intermediate class. As a fat person in his early forties who didn't know the first thing about swimming, he sluggishly moved to the side of the pool, rubbed water on his chest, and fumbled into the pool, holding onto the ladder like the other women.

"Did you change classes?" his wife asked him that evening. He answered in a serious tone.

"They have a funny policy. They said they couldn't change it since I'd already signed up."

"What? That's nonsense. Cancel it."

"Well, I don't think we should go that far."

"Honey, do you know how much it is? It's seventy thousand won. Seventy thousand. I'll do it."

"No, no. I gave it a try today, and it turns out I forgot all the strokes. I think starting at the basic level will be OK."

"Well, now that just seems weird. You were so against exercising."

"Today, I really saw how necessary exercise is."

The next morning, he bolted out of bed even before his wife woke him up and speedily drove to the health club. The majority of the class was young women with office jobs. It was difficult for housewives to make the early morning class because they were busy preparing breakfast. There were no men. He paddled enthusiastically while pondering the mystery of what the men of the world were doing instead of exercising, particularly instead of swimming in the early morning beginner's class.

"OK, let's go underwater now. Whoever holds their breath the longest gets a prize. Put your arms around the shoulders of the person next to you. All ready? Everybody go!"

Following the instructor's cue, he submerged himself under water. On one side, he saw a young lady who looked about twenty, while on the other side a woman who looked about thirty was putting her arm on his shoulder. Regardless of their age, he felt quite blissful. From that day on, he didn't miss a single day of class, come snow or rain or wind. On Sundays, when there were no classes, he was impossibly bored. He didn't even feel alive. His wife was truly taken aback by this.

"You really find swimming that enjoyable?"

"No, not really."

"Then why are you so into it?"

"I told you. I need the exercise. Plus, just think of how much the lessons cost. It's so wasteful to miss even one day."

"Exercising really works, doesn't it?"

"Yep."

"Maybe I should also take classes next month."

He was so surprised that an "agh" got caught up in his throat, and he fiercely waved his hand.

"No way. You'll get anemic if you swim. You're already too skinny as you are."

"Skinny? I can feel my gut starting to develop."

"Woman, you can start when your gut is as big as mine."

"You're looking slim these days. It seems it took less than a month for your potbelly to slim down."

"No, I've still got a long way to go. It'll take months of hard work at least."

One month passed, and then another, but he stayed in the beginner's class. But something strange happened. Even when he did try swimming seriously, he realized he'd lost the ability to swim beyond the beginner's level.

THE GHOST-CATCHING
CIVIL SERVICE GUARD

THIS IS A story from ten years ago, of a happy guy who served his conscript duty as an off-base guard performing civil services. He was quite cocky for a civil service guard back in those times, enjoying the privilege of driving a car to and from work, which wouldn't have been possible had he been a regular conscript. Although it was a deteriorating vehicle with a hole in the floor for air-conditioning, it was nonetheless useful for driving to work over the steep hill called Fox's Hill.

One summer night, he was driving back home. At the top of the hill, through the rain, he could see a person dressed in white holding up a hand. He was sure that the person standing before his headlights was a young woman. This had always been his dream scenario and he yelled for joy as he slowed down his car. The woman, soaked in rain, was even prettier than he'd expected. She had a doleful beauty about her. A few strands of hair covered her face and she looked exactly like the girl of his dreams, with her half-closed eyes and parted lips, but he nevertheless felt the hairs on his back stand up. There was no way a woman standing alone on a deserted hill at night, and in the rain no less, was in her right mind.

He stopped his car anyway. He rolled down his window just enough for his voice to be heard and asked in a nervous voice, "Do you need a ride?"

The beautiful and frightful woman nodded her head, a blank expression on her face. She then extended her long, pale hand to grab the door handle. Quickly locking the doors, he said in a shaky voice, "But you know, it's nighttime and this is a hill known to be haunted by mythical foxes. Not to mention that it's raining, you know? Could you show me some ID?"

The woman just stood still for a while before she silently opened her soaked handbag with her soaked hands and took our her soaked ID card, handing it over to him through the open window. With trembling hands, he took a good look at both sides of the card and the photo. He decided that ghosts or mythical foxes wouldn't have ID cards and so he let her in.

As soon as she took a seat, the car was filled with the scent of a woman's skin still wet from the rain. The civil service guard felt like his nose was burning and that he'd go blind, but he kept his senses by clutching the steering wheel with all his might.

"Where to?" he asked, clenching his teeth to keep his sanity.

"Just to the bridge. There'll be a bus there."

She had an accent that was rare in the downtown area where he lived. It was a subtle country accent with a classic ring that could be heard only in cozy, rural villages, and it drove him crazy. He thought to himself, "So what if she's a ghost? Or a mythical fox? I might as well hang myself if I don't marry this woman."

"Oh, that's great, we're going in the same direction. I'll give you a ride home."

The woman opened her mouth, her lips as red as roses even without any lipstick on.

"Is that the way you were going?"

He started talking as he slowly stretched out his hand in her direction.

"Miss," he said, laughing, "I may seem otherwise, but I'm a gentleman of chivalry. You think I'd let a lady travel alone this late at night? It shouldn't matter if that's the direction I was going in or not. By the way, are you married? Of course, there's no way you are. And thankfully, neither am I. The heavens have poured down rain and allowed us to meet, so that the two of us can get married. So, accordingly, I'm going to meet your parents today and introduce myself. What kind of gift do you think they'd like? Maybe your father appreciates liquor. Yes, rice wine would be good."

He even slipped an arm over her shoulder as he spoke, but the woman didn't budge, only looking ahead, showing the side of her elegant face. With no one to tell him to stop, he became even more audacious.

"I didn't have many brothers or sisters, so I'm thinking we'll have many kids, but I'm a little worried because you look frail. That's OK. We'll take it slow. I'm off duty tomorrow, so let's get together and talk in the morning. Oh, and what should we do about the ring?"

That's when the woman opened her mouth.

"This is the bridge. Please stop the car."

He had no intention of doing so. His head was filled with blueprints of their future and a sense of duty to introduce himself to his in-laws.

"No, no. There's no way to know when the bus will come. I said I'm going to drive you. It's to the left, right?"

He'd taken note of the address when he checked her ID card on the hill. He made a grand gesture of turning the car around in the direction of the address, just like it was a scene out of a movie. The woman still didn't respond in any way.

"Are your parents home tonight?"

"They're not at home now. I'm alone."

"Oh, no. I really wanted to introduce myself to them."

He silently cried out "Yes!" and didn't know how to contain his excitement.

"Do you really want to introduce yourself?"

She stared at him with eyes that shone like grapes. He scratched the back of his head as he answered.

"Sure, of course."

"They're not at home, but my father's around here somewhere. Would you like to say hi to him now?"

He nodded his head, feeling a little bit reluctant. The woman told him to pull over. When he did, she got out of the car. After making sure he was out of the car too, she cupped her hands around her mouth and shouted toward the pitch-dark forest.

"Dad! Dad!"

He glared at the forest through the rainfall but could see nothing except several round grave mounds that were caught in the light of his headlights. Suddenly, he felt beads of sweat, not rain, trickling down his back. The woman shouted into the darkness, an echo carrying her sorrow.

"Dad! Dad! I'm here! Mom's well! Mom says she misses you! I miss you, too! Why are you just lying there? Please get up now, Dad! Your little girl's here!"

Although it was missing the howling of foxes and some flying ghosts, the place was no doubt a graveyard. The goose bumps all over his skin made it nearly impossible for him to move his body, but as a fully-trained civil service guard, he mustered up every ounce of energy left in him and jumped into his car. He didn't even think about looking back as he sped away at full speed. After the hill came a village. He breathed a sigh of relief, having made it there alive, as he pulled up to a store in the middle of the village. On the wide wooden bench at the storefront were some old men from the neighborhood sitting around with drinks. He opened the fridge in the store to grab a soda and quickly gulped down the bottle. He asked the old men what the neighborhood was called. It was indeed the name of the village that'd been written on the ID card of the beautiful, mythical fox ghost.

"Do you know if this woman lives here?"

He described the woman and said her name. Each of the old men chimed in with what they knew, telling him that not only had the young woman been born and raised there, but that she still lived there.

"She lives here? Where?"

"It's that big house with the jujube tree. Oh, but the poor girl. She lost both parents in the span of a month, so it's no wonder she's been acting a bit strange . . ."

He bought the biggest bottle of soju from the store. He got to the woman's house before she did, and while he waited for her he drank out of the bottle. The next day and the day after that, he repeated this ritual around the same time. In time, the woman recovered from her emotional problems and, a few months after that, married him.

The guy currently lives a busy life as the father of two boys and three girls. His wife's still stunning and makes a lovely home, rearing the kids with toughness and sweetness, along with her husband, who still follows her around everywhere.

TO BURY ONE'S HEAD

SOME TICKS ARE parasitic on the bodies of dogs. Catch a dog scratching itself like crazy and look through its fur. With its head buried in the tender flesh of a dog, the tick sucks on its blood. It lacks a neck, and it's hard to tell where its stomach ends and tail begins. The male is about 2.5 millimeters long and the female about 7.5 millimeters long. Unless you use tweezers to carefully pull it out, it'll break. Once a tick buries its head, it refuses to come back out. It'll die trying to get deeper inside. This phenomenon is what I'd like to call, "to bury one's head in something."

THE AMUSING LIFE - 1

DEAR NEW MEMBERS. You have solemnly sworn on the great altar of lies that you will give your life and last drop of blood for the day that truth becomes falsity and falsity becomes truth. On behalf of the twenty billion members and fifty thousand senators, twenty thousand tribunes, seven thousand consuls, one hundred and ninety-five thousand four hundred financiers, forty-three thousand inspectors, one hundred and twenty thousand judges, and five thousand viceroys of the World Wide Liars Confederation, I welcome you with all my heart and would like to offer you a few words of advice.

The list of great liars in history includes most kings, historians, lawyers, priests, and scientists. If you don't believe this, try reading Thucydides, Herodotus, Tacitus, Marco Polo, Machiavelli, or take note of the lives of conquerors such as Alexander the Great, Genghis Khan, Napoleon, Attila,or Qin Shi Huang. (Personally, I'd just believe what I'm saying and skip reading and studying all of that.) Learning to deceive the public and to strategically fool the enemy, to bring victory and glory to oneself, is what history's all about.

Thankfully, you're not tasked with creating history like the aforementioned heroes of the past. All you need to do, as extraordinary liars in your own lives, is to pursue your small responsibilities, to make peace and joy in your everyday lives. Among you are novelists, cartoonists, actors, artists, managers, critics, advertisers, soldiers, athletes, businessmen, spies, and anchormen—or persons aspiring to be those things. Depending on how well and realistically you lie, how well you fool others, you'll receive compliments and live successful lives. Have no suspicions against each other, as there are no politicians among you. Nor are there any of their dregs—deputies, waiters who work at summit meetings, oversophisticated ambassadors of international unions. They'll dishonor our titles as liars with their transparent lies. There are no economists, mathematicians, nuclear scientists, and astrologers among us either. The false truth they believe in and advocate for is far more evil than any true lie, and may misguide people.

Ladies and gentlemen. What is a lie? A lie embellishes our lives and expands our imagination to universal heights. A lie is like the custard cream that hides inside the hard bread of truth, providing unexpected delight, sweet stories that melt in your mouth. A life without lies is like a pair of panties without its elastic waistband, or an elastic waistband without panties to be fitted to it.

The first recorded human lie was a cave painting, in Spain, dating back thirty-five thousand years. It's a painting of a hunter strangling a mammoth. One of our predecessors, a cheeky liar, probably imagined that a mammoth was something the size of a frog and told his buddies, who'd never seen a mammoth before, that he beat it with a stick until it died. One of his buddies, an artist who believed him, slightly embellished the story and drew a picture of several men hunting a baby mammoth. After some time passed, a younger artist with a strong sense of responsibility completed the world's first lie by drawing a lone hunter strangling a large male mammoth, right next to the earlier painting.

Contrary to the pictures, modern paleontologists say mammoths didn't exist in warm areas south of the Alps. Let all of us, as descendants of those great ancestors who've left behind that cave painting, and as contemporaries of the paleontologist, figure out who's telling the best lie.

OK, how can we tell a good lie? A semi-member of our association from a century ago, American writer Mark Twain, lied by saying there were 869 types of lies (that would be 870 types, including his own lie), but no matter the number of types, the common and essential element of a lie is a good memory. A person with a bad memory can't become even the most elementary liar. A true liar must be able to relentlessly lie until he himself believes it's the truth. To do so, he must remember the previous lie he told before it. He must remember not only the content, but the tone, response, emotion, accent, nuance, and even the gestures, to gain recognition as a liar.

Next, and this may be a bit difficult to comprehend for those of you who just broke out of your shell, but it's important when you lie to leave room for your audience to think, so that they may interpret it in one way or another. Look at the vulgar fortune-tellers who walk the same paths as ours, but open up shop on any part of that road, no different than swindlers. The slick ones never speak in a conclusive manner. They speak in a vague manner—for example, "Sirius has intruded Polaris from the North, and there will be bad news from a faraway land"—so that the listener will interpret it to fit his own situation, and the fortune-teller won't be held responsible afterward. "I absolutely, exactly, surely, clearly, swear on it with my life . . ." If you utter these absurd words, then I absolutely, exactly, surely, clearly, swear on it with my life, that you will not become a great liar.

And when arguing about falsity and truth, if you're to win with falsity then there must be no possibility of counter-evidence. The trick is to say something like "just between you and me" (when nobody else knows about it), or to attribute it to someone who's already dead (since the dead can't speak), or borrow the mouth of someone who has the same interest as us, or leak it through the mouth of the enemy (because nobody will believe the enemy).

To the infants who've just entered the world of great lies: you should not be ashamed of lying. Lying is an innate function. Human speech has lies in it anyway. What we acquire and are forced to learn is the lie of the moral rule that we shouldn't lie. Is there a reason we should be ashamed of the way we're born? When someone tells you, "Don't lie," you must be able to instantly lie and answer, "OK, I won't," to become a true liar. Some people find joy in spreading lies, despite the danger of facing great embarrassment when caught. Take my driver, for instance. Even when he's not been paid his overtime compensation, he will lie without even so much as blinking an eye, saying he's already been paid, just to stay true to his impulse to lie. This is, incidentally, quite helpful for the budget of the association.

Extra notes. There is the pure lie, the stinking lie, and the true lie which always begins with "Statistics say . . ." (This latter is attributed to the English politician and infamous liar, Disraeli, but it can't be found in any part of his book of quotations. Despite this, because Mark Twain lied about Disraeli having said it, a few stupid generals have quoted him as saying so.) And we recognize the lie that a lie that answers to moral truth, which is of a higher level than truth based on fact, is a non-lie. Nature is also our friend, a liar. The earth claims to be round, but it expresses itself always as being flat. The earth claims to be circling the sun, but it acts as if the sun circled it.

My fellow members, there hasn't yet been a mastermind who's lied from birth to death through every thought, utterance, action, plan and execution. There are only people who've come close. Rather than living like a fool in a half-wit world that's perfectly filled with neither truth nor lies, let us live thrilling and amusing lives as true liars.

Long live lies. Long live the Worldwide Liars Association. Go on forever, history of lies.

From the last prince of the kingdom of Sabeol, friend of all who are poor, the world's best poet, prophet, magician, captain of the 2002 grand exploration team of Lake Baikal, researcher of the Chinese language in the time of Nan-Bei Chao, secretary of the 96th zone of Citizens Who Want To Become Good Fathers, owner of Geumjeong high-tech dry cleaners ("We hope to see you soon!"), general secretary of the World Wide Liars Confederation (WWLC). In the year two million six hundred seventy-five since the origin of lies.

AN ORANGE FLAVORED ORANGE

B WAS A newbie to the editing department. He was in charge of design but as we were a publishing company he was more knowledgeable about the Korean language than designers in any other business. The problem however was that everything he knew was a little off. And instead of admitting his errors, he'd choose to irritate us by doubting the dictionary or members of the editing department who made a living with those dictionaries in hand. So whenever he'd make a mistake, we got revenge by changing his nickname to a word that symbolized the mistake. Let me give you an example.

"B. What are you doing? It's still early in the work day, shouldn't you be working?"

"Sir. Those are killer legs on that lady standing in front of that office supply store. The agony's killing me."

"B. This design is yours right? If you liked the word 'killer' so much, why didn't you just change the phrase "strong inundation" in the description to 'killer inundation'?"

"Mrs. M," he replied, laughing, "your legs are also quite killer, but that lady seems to be at least a decade younger than you. Accordingly, uhm, jealousy is one of the seven great sins a wife can commit . . ."

"What kind of crap is that!"

For a while, his nickname was "killer inundation." By a while, I mean until the "intersecting" incident took place a few months later.

Summer had come and so did high school baseball season. B was avidly cheering on the team of a school that was from his hometown, but just because it was from his hometown and not because he'd gone to that school. It didn't seem like he ever went to a game, just rooted for the team on television or kept up through reading the newspaper.

"Oh, wow! Sir, yesterday the pitcher of our Gyungshin Industrial High School team hit consecutive homeruns. The catcher had four hits in six at-bats, and the shortstop stole four bases. They're no doubt going to the finals."

"Listen, B. You went to a normal high school. In your hometown, did you just have to attend a similarly named school to be considered alumni?"

"Sir," he giggled, "you're in the dark. The city of Gyungshin is the permanent capital of Korean baseball, wouldn't you say? When you hear baseball, you think of Gyungshin, and vice versa."

That's when M entered the conversation.

"Then why didn't they name the city Baseball? Actually, from now on, in honor of your hometown, B, we'll call you Baseball."

Any other person would've retreated by then, but everything was smooth sailing with B.

"I see I only have enemies on all sides. I can hear the Chu kingdom's song from all sides. Alas!"

"B, let me ask you something. Do you know why the enemy sings the song from the Chu kingdom in the story?"

"Mrs. M, I guess it's because you're a woman, but you don't know your history that well. I'll tell you. You see, Xiang Yu was surrounded by Liu Bang's army during the Battle of Red Cliffs."

"I think you mean Gaixia, not Red Cliffs."

"Sir, it's not important to know whether it was Gaixia or Red Cliffs. The important thing is that the army of the Han dynasty couldn't help but learn the popular song from the kingdom of Chu while surrounding them for so long. After listening to that song and realizing he'd lost, Xiang Yu killed himself because the song made him so sad."

"Are you saying that the Han army sung a Chu dynasty song?"

"That's right. That was Liu Bang's strategy all along. Sir, why do you insist on breaking up the story just when things are about to get intersecting?"

"Things are about to get what?"

"See, you're doing it again."

"B, I didn't hear you either. Say it again?"

"Oh, intersecting!"

"Intersecting?"

"Intersecting! Why? What's wrong with that?"

After earning the nickname "intersecting" instead of "the gentleman of all things baseball," B laid low for a while, as if to show signs of improvement or, in his terms, "improvidence." Then one day, he got married. He dated in such secrecy that nobody knew what was going on, and out of the blue got married. It was so sudden that some of our coworkers couldn't even attend the wedding. Feeling bad about this, the ones who didn't attend bought some orange juice as a housewarming gift when we all visited his home.

"Hey, why don't you bring us something to drink?"

He hadn't even been married a month and yet he acted as if he'd been bossing his wife around for a decade. It was as if not doing so would make him look bad. His wife appeared, looking like a woman who had been through it all, selling goods at a street market, disappointing those who were anticipating a blushing new bride. Adding to that, the drinks that his wife brought out earned B a new nickname.

"The orange juice that I bought was the expensive kind, one hundred percent natural, no sugar added. Somehow in the kitchen it transformed into cheap orange-flavored soda. What a fantastic couple.

"The moment the group left his house, everybody agreed to call him "orange flavor" for a while." And his wife, who'd enjoy hundred percent orange juice, would be referred to as Mrs. Orange.

THE LEGEND

IT'S BEEN QUITE a while, but even now, I can recall the details of his appearance. His tangled hair, shabby clothes made of sturdy and dirt-repelling fabric, his habit of schlepping, the unhealthy looking dark tone of his skin, thick lips, a long and high-bridged nose. Maybe the reason I came to store the picture of this, guy, who was like any average guy hanging out at the pool hall, in my memory was the fact that he was a player who'd reached the elusive level of one thousand points, which was a legendary feat back then. Around that time, I'd accumulated ten years of experience in the sport but my level hadn't budged from two hundred, which was the same level I'd been on since graduating from school. However, the reason I remember him even now has to be his face, his blank, expressionless face.

In the world of four-ball billiards, which is at once a sport, a form of entertainment, as well as a war field of victory or defeat, there are countless words like push, pull, suck, flip, peel, give, and spin, which could all be construed as somewhat sexual if heard by a novice. Colorful gestures, shouts, exclamations, pleas, begging, and expressions of joy accompany the "ah"s that escape lips when a ball that was supposed to hit actually misses, the "Come on!"s that stem from the jealousy that arises when your opponent gets a lucky hit, and the prayers for one's ball to go through and not one's opponent's. However, none of this could be found in him. He was always amazingly expressionless. If one could rank facial expressions that display the various feelings, degrees of greed, forms of passion humans possess, his expressionless face would probably rise above them all.

One muggy summer evening, I witnessed an interesting sight when, dragging my summer sandals, I stopped by the pool hall, which was barely a bus stop away from my house. A particularly chatty fellow who was a salaried worker at some company and also a regular at the pool hall was in the midst of a match with him. This chatty fellow claimed to be at a level of five hundred points, but the way he'd never shut up while playing the game always made me think that the thirty-something-year-old was probably at a level similar to mine. The chatty fellow's colleagues surrounded the table, holding their breath, and my friend who owned the pool hall had his arms crossed, wearing a significant look.

"What's going on?"

"They provoked the sleeping lion . . ."

It seemed that the chatty fellow who'd won a game amongst his colleagues asked the thousand-point legend if he could learn a thing or two from him. When the legend declined, the chatty fellow felt he'd been blown off, so he challenged him to a bet rather than a friendly game. "How are we to believe that you have a thousand points on you if we've never seen you play? There's no guarantee that a bogus thousand points will win against a genuine five hundred pointer." The chatty fellow loudly emphasized these points to his colleagues and told them that he himself had lived the pool hall life somewhere in Yeosu, somewhere in Ulsan, and somewhere in Youngdeungpo. Perhaps he shouldn't have said, "I was crawling at the lowest point of my life" as he talked about what a pathetic and laughable life it was, and how poor and miserable he'd been. After all, even a pathetic, impoverished person who was just killing time, and his spirit along with it, in a suburban neighborhood pool hall has his pride. We didn't know whether it was the bet that was proposed or the critical comments about his pathetic life that made him take up the challenge, but he did.

A "military discharge" four-ball billiards game was already in progress between the two when I set foot in the pool hall. The game was, of course, played on a bet, and the chatty fellow unhesitatingly suggested to the poor thousand-point legend that they bet an amount equivalent to what would be given as a summer bonus payment back in those days. The legend had no cash, but the owner of the pool hall, my friend, who'd spent quite a long time with the legend, lent him the money. And the game was on.

I wasn't familiar with the world of legends, but even for someone like me, it was exciting to watch one player continuously exclaim, sigh, complain, and curse, while the other player invariably hit the ball and waited, standing completely still with an unchanging, blank stare. It wasn't just the talking. Whenever the chatty fellow hit the ball and tilted over like a millet stalk, as his eyes chased the ball his colleagues would bend over and stand back up in the same way, shouting out ha's and huh's, and sometimes even producing a burst of applause. As the game progressed, there was more blatant cheering, as well as gestures and booing. The only people cheering for the legend, who kept on in silence with a blank face, were my friend, who'd lent him the money, and myself, naturally inclined to side with the underdog.

As the game became more exciting, there came an opportunity for the legend, who'd been playing a losing game up to that point, to turn it around. According to my friend's commentary, holding his breath in the corner and watching, this was the ball

that could end the game. However, for some reason he didn't hit
the ball. One minute and then another passed, and the spectators' whispering was hushed. Even the chatty fellow stopped his
relentless chatting and, nervously shaking his thighs, looked by
turns at the ball and then at the legend. When even that shaking
had subsided, the legend held up his cue. The route he chose for
the ball was a surprisingly difficult one, which sent the ball in
full-spin around the table.

Having gone around the table, the ball's momentum had
almost died out before it reached the ball it was aimed at.
Hoping the ball wouldn't hit the mark, the chatty fellow raised
his chin as high as he could, his body squirming. The spectators
were all in identical poses like a row of birds on a wire. Hoping
the ball would hit, I had my chin out as far as possible, when my
eyes fell on his face across the table. It was still expressionless. His
eyes were fixed on the ball moving toward him, but that was it,
no change. His face was exactly as it was before he hit the ball.

When the ball brushed past the other ball ever so lightly,
victory became clear. The chatty fellow paid his money. After
he and his entourage left noisily, only the three of us remained.

"That last shot seemed to be the deciding shot . . . why did
he choose such a difficult route?"

"To make sure that even if he didn't get it, there wouldn't be a
possible angle for his opponent either. That's how legends do it."

After talking a bit, we decided that we'd go for a beer and
my friend got ready to close up the pool hall. As we waited, the
legend took his shoes off and fanned his foot. Something strange
caught my eye. His socks had holes where his big toe was.

"Curious?"

My friend, who was somehow by my side again, gave me
the answer.

"Legends can't show they're nervous on the outside. Instead, they wiggle their toes inside their shoes and that's what ends up happening to their socks."

The expressionless legend finally showed the faintest smile as he opened his pouch bag. He took out socks, a towel, toothbrush, soap and what not, and put the money he'd just collected inside. The socks that came out of the bag all had large holes in the same big toe spot.

WHY PLUMS ARE RED

I HAVE NO intention of arguing about which is the king among fruits. But if someone asks me which fruit most resembles an adorable newborn prince, I'd say a plum. This fruit is born on plum trees, which are a deciduous tree species belonging to the rose tree family. The flowers of this tree come to bloom around April, and three months afterward it bears a fruit that has a red exterior and a sweet and tangy yellow flesh.

It's enough to recall the following saying when it comes to discussing how delicious nectars are: "Don't adjust your hat strings under an oyat tree and don't adjust your shoe straps in a melon patch." Oyat is another name for a plum.

There was a farmhouse that belonged to an older friend of mine that I used to visit when I had some writing to do. Near the stream in front of the house stood a plum tree. Across the stream was a pen for an elk, and the elk resembled the deer in the movie *The Deer Hunter*. The size of the elk inside the pen allows you to estimate the wealth of the owner. It also lets you vaguely guess the taste or character of the person. What sort of character is that, you ask?

The elk is more expensive than the average cow. Cows yield milk or meat. It can also be made to pull plows or carry yoke. But the elk? It produces neither milk nor meat nor strength, only a bucketful of flies every day from its pen. So why would one raise an elk? Because its long neck makes one have compassion for it? Because the owner is an animal activist? Because he carries an injured soul from the Vietnam War? Just because? None of the above. The elk yields its large horns. Although they're both in the same family, the Formosan deer only produces horns the size of your finger, while the elk can give you horns as large as a shovel. So you see that an owner of the elk is out to strike it big. If he's going to raise something, why not aim for one easy, big profit? That's what I suspect.

The last name of the owner of the house behind the pen is "Go." So I call him Mr. Go. Unlike my friend's house, which holds up a slate roof with clay walls, the neighbor's house is a proud modern-style house built a few years back with an investment of nearly two million won per 3.3 square meters. A handsome brown roof that comes with a chimney for a fireplace, a wall with a huge glass panel, and a pond with goldfish swimming in it—all would make you want to guess the occupation of Mr. Go and his family. In any case, Mr. Go is a farmer. The other houses in the neighborhood are summerhouses that are even fancier than Mr. Go's house, but it's said that Mr. Go takes care of these properties as well. He mows and waters the lawn, and even glares at those who snoop about. Of course, he probably gets paid for his troubles.

Anyway, let's get back to talking about the stream between my friend's house and his neighbor's, and the plum tree that stood there. Behind the plum tree stands the deer pen, and beyond that is a peach orchard.

What's your opinion of peaches? In my opinion, the peach is the queen of all fruit. The flower of a peach tree is pink or like a salmon-red, and there's no other flower that's as beautiful. Only after the peach flowers bloom is spring a true sight to see.

It's almost as if spring got its name from the phrase, "the peach flowers springing from every branch." And summer? I say the season got its name from the "sumptuousness of all peaches" from which it becomes "sumptuous -> summer." Based on the same logic, eating a peach is "the joy of living in this world," taking a peach from its tree is "like taking the world in your hand," and gazing at a peach is "what it feels like to gaze at the world." The early summer peach, which begins to show splashes of red, is as graceful as a young princess, while a fully ripe red peach presents a seductive flavor undetectable in other fruits, with all of its succulent juices and plush pulp. Perhaps much like that princess who seduced a high ranking monk long ago.

It was July when I visited my friend's house, just when the peaches in the orchards were beginning to change to red. I admired the grace of the princess and decided to eat the peach joyfully and happily. The orchards have an owner and the trees, in addition to the peaches on it, have an owner as well.

In a reasonable world, one should find the owner of the orchard and say, "I've decided I want to eat a peach at about eight o'clock tonight."

Then the owner would say, "The peaches aren't ripe yet."

I'd say, "That's exactly what I want to eat: a peach just beginning to turn red. It's just that royal grace-like quality that I'd like to taste."

"You can't pick the peaches before they're ripe. That's my decision and also what nature requires of each peach."

"Regardless, I'd like to eat a peach."

"Then go ahead. Eat however much you want, and consider the orchard as your own. Help yourself for free."

How wonderful it would be if the conversation went as such. But most owners of peaches, especially Mr. Go, wouldn't like it. As such, my resolution to pay the owner of the orchard a visit disappeared.

Nevertheless, I couldn't get rid of the desire to eat a peach. Plus, I couldn't resist the fun of a peach heist, which I hadn't experienced in a long, long time. What really got to me was the "win big" philosophy of the elk's owner. In the name of all deer hunters, for the pride of cows everywhere, as revenge for the swarm of flies that came out of the deer pen, I armed myself and headed for the orchard at dusk.

As soon as I entered the orchard, a mysterious, long, yawn-like sound tickled my ears. I fell flat on the ground. I was over-whelmed by the smell of manure. Then I heard the long yawn-like sound again. It was the cry of a deer in heat. There I added another reason to the list of reasons I was on this peach heist. I had to endure this ghastly sound the whole time.

Finally, I had in my hand the royal princess of all fruits, the peach, which brings spring and summer to the world. I could feel the prickly fur. The thing that you need to watch out for during a peach heist is this fur, which is just as prim as prim can be. If you happen to touch it the wrong way, the prickliness and itchiness will make you forget about any royal princess or getting your money's worth. I carefully pocketed the peaches, and with lightning speed returned to our yard to bathe the royal princesses in spring water. That's when I heard my friend call out from the room.

"What in the world are you doing?"

"Sleeping."

"If you're sleeping, why do I hear water?"

"Maybe fairies came down to the earth and they're bathing in the stream."

I ate eight peaches that night.

The next day, I was returning from an errand and I noticed someone standing under the plum tree. It was Mr. Go. He kept picking the plums as if he hadn't noticed I was there. I was ready to yell at him with clenched fists, "why are you picking someone else's plums?" when right then, near my feet, I saw the scattered peach seeds I'd thrown away the day before.

Ah, so the industrious fellow counted the number of peaches in his orchard this morning. He realized that eight of his peaches had gone missing and probably thought that I was the only one who was capable of committing such a crime. Not having any evidence, he came to confirm his suspicion and found the peach seeds on the ground. He decided to wait for me while picking some plums, silently telling himself that if I so much as spoke a word, he'd grab me by the collar. And he continued picking fruit, pretending not to have a care in the world.

So I had no choice but to think this over. The truth is that a stream doesn't belong to anybody. Technically, a plum tree standing near a stream that doesn't belong to anybody, doesn't belong to anybody either. The prince of fruit, the blood-red plum, ready to burst out of its seams, hangs on a plum tree which doesn't belong to anybody, and so also doesn't belong to anybody . . .

Not indicating whether he knew these things or not, or whether he even thought about them, Mr. Go continued to pick the plums. He took a bowlful and handed it to me. I took this as a sign of reconciliation. The great reconciliation of the princess and prince of fruit. I thanked him, and Mr. Go let out a hearty laugh. He told me not to mention it and proceeded to saunter toward his house with three bowlfuls of plums.

About an hour later my friend returned home. I gave him one of the washed plums.

"It's good. Did you pick them?"

"Not me. Mr. Go picked them and gave me some."

This sent my friend into a rage.

"Go? Why?"

"Doesn't that tree belong to him?" I asked, with a plum as red as deer's blood in my mouth.

"Listen, man, that's our land."

"That deer pen is Mr. Go's, isn't it? If the tree's closer to that side, doesn't that make it his?"

"The deer pen belongs to the old man Park down the road."

I kept silent for a moment. But I just had to ask one last question.

"Then who owns the orchard?"

He kicked one of the young peach seeds, the princesses I'd eaten and discarded the night before.

"That's old man Park's, too."

SHORT-LEASHED

WHEN SHE BECAME pregnant, his wife had unusually severe morning sickness. It seemed her bump was much bigger than other pregnant women's as well. As the pounds rapidly piled on, she didn't like to move. She was very thin and frail to begin with, so the couple talked to the doctor about whether a natural birth was a possibility, but the doctor gave them an indefinite answer, saying he'd have to see at the time of delivery.

"A natural birth is the best," the husband would say. "When I see women who can't take even that much pain and opt for a Cesarean, I wonder whether or not they have what it takes to become mothers. When I was in combat training back in the military . . ."

Every chance he got, he'd go on about his experience receiving military training that far exceeded human endurance, and how humans were designed to far exceed their abilities in extreme situations. He'd also bring home books on abdominal breathing or painless childbirth to encourage his wife to choose natural childbirth. Despite the time and money he spent, his wife was terrified before entering the delivery room.

"Honey, you can do it, right? You can do it. I know you can. Go! Lee Sook-Hee!"

He followed alongside the rolling bed with a clenched fist, trying to psych her up. Amidst squirming from the intermittent pain that came to her, she turned around to look at him and whispered that she'd just think of it as going to the military and that she'd give it her best shot. After sitting on the bench in front of the delivery room for three hours, listening to painful cries coming from the room, he couldn't take it anymore, so he went and guzzled down several beers at a liquor store near the hospital. Another three hours had passed. He went to the store again and came back after having chugged down a bottle of soju. A nurse emerged from the room and told him to come in. He tried to steady his footing as he entered the delivery room.

"Honey, I can't take it anymore. Please let me have a Cesarean, please?"

He felt his heart sink, but he pulled himself together.

"Just try it once more. Let's do it together. I'm standing right outside that door. Don't worry and try it. The doctor said he'd do a Cesarean if he needed to. Just one last time, one last time."

His wife pleaded with him in tears, but with a clenched jaw he shook his head. Even the doctor said they'd try one last time and then consider a Cesarean. He squeezed his wife's hand once more before stepping out. While his wife was giving it everything she had, he fell asleep on the chair, thinking about the pain he'd felt the time he broke his shoulder during combat training in the military.

His wife succeeded on the last try. It was a boy. However, in that very dramatic and moving moment, he was asleep. It was the moment for him to run over to his wife and hold her shoulders, tell her that she did well, that he loved her, but he missed the chance. Damned sleep. His mother-in-law didn't even think of waking him, as she ran into the room and conveyed to his wife, who was just coming back to her senses, that her husband was snoring. As if that were some kind of good news. His wife used this story against him time and time again afterward.

"Having ten mouths wouldn't do you any good because you have no excuse. You said 'no' to a Cesarean when I begged you, and then you doze off while I'm screaming, in the throes of life and death?"

He was about to stammer out an apology, that he only drank because he loved her so much, that he couldn't bear the anxiety that came with worrying so much about the baby and her, but then he decided that he'd take a different tack. His wife wasn't the kind of person to understand if he talked to her reasonably. Buying her a bouquet of roses would be much more effective. He'd made a critical mistake but he consoled himself with the fact that he'd also scored an important gain. If she'd gotten a Cesarean section, she'd have to go through the same operation when she had another child, but he'd prevented such an undesirable situation from happening.

"I sometimes have strange thoughts. I really think that I have five children and only one of them is out in this world."

He told her of his thoughts one day on the way to a nearby park, holding the hands of his toddler, who was walking quite steadily now. And he received great news: one of the kids whom he'd believed existed somewhere was then growing inside his wife's womb. However, his wife made sure of things beforehand this time around.

"This time, you sign the operation papers beforehand, or else I'm not having this baby. If you tell me to bear it like last time, you can forget about having a kid."

He was too ecstatic to think seriously about the ramifications of what she was saying. He held his child high in the air and shouted, "Joohyun, it's a baby! You're getting a little brother or sister."

Not to repeat his mistake, he quit drinking altogether as their due date approached. While folding the adorable baby clothes, his wife told her mother, who came to help watch the baby, that they wouldn't have to worry too much since they were going to have a Cesarean this time.

"He doesn't want more kids?"

"Mom, who has more than two kids these days? That's just his wishful thinking."

"But he keeps saying that more is better, like three or four . . ."

"Mom, you can still have one or two after you've had a Cesarean. He knows that, too."

He was jumping rope in the yard when he overheard mother and daughter talking, and he secretly smiled. On her due date, his wife checked into the hospital and without any protest, he stamped his name on the forms.

The waiting area in front of the delivery room was especially crowded that day. There weren't many men like him, as it was mostly elderly people, pregnant women, and children. As a man with prior experience, he leisurely sat in a chair, reading the papers.

Once in a while, a bed carrying a mother went in, and guys who looked about three or four years younger than he was nervously followed the bed shouting, "Hang in there! We're almost there!" Every time this happened, he nodded and leafed through his papers. He went out to smoke a cigarette for a short while but everything was the same when he came back. The operation would start at the scheduled time and end at the scheduled time. His mother-in-law held their firstborn child and was making small talk with other grandmothers about this and that. He was satisfied that everything was going smoothly. Just then, a young nurse came out and yelled, "Where is the guardian for Lee Sook-Hee?"

Instantly, everybody in the hall looked to the nurse, but as they realized it didn't concern them they went back to their business. He quickly got up and approached the nurse.

"That's me. Did she have the baby?"

"Congratulations, it's a princess."

He could tell other people stopped their conversations to shoot envious looks his way. He nodded his head in satisfaction and turned to his mother-in-law.

"Mother, it's a girl."

"Oh, God. Thank you so much."

His mother-in-law drew a cross across her chest.

"Is this their first?" an elderly person next to her asked.

"No, it's their second. This one's their first."

"One boy and one girl. You're so lucky. My daughter-in-law had a daughter and another daughter and is going through all this trouble to have a son."

"I see."

His mother-in-law was contemplating saying something, before turning her head away. Right then, a nurse shoved some papers in his face.

"You have your stamp, right? Please stamp your name right there."

"What's this?"

Surprised, he suddenly yelled. He'd already stamped his name. If he was being asked to do it again, did that mean they were having twins?

"Since we already have her open, we're going to go ahead and perform sterilization. A lot of people do it."

"What?"

He jumped in protest. There were still children to be had, and they were talking about sterilization?

The old woman who'd said her daughter-in-law had two daughters carefully asked him, "This baby you just had is a daughter, right?"

Annoyed that the old woman was unexpectedly butting into their business, he haughtily answered, "Yes, so?"

The old woman interrogated him in yes or no form, as if he were at a hearing.

"You have an older son?"

"Yes."

"So having a daughter today means you have one boy and one girl."

"What did I just say?"

"Then why are you being so greedy? Do you even know how much pain women go through having children? Giving birth isn't even half of it. What about taking care of them? Men . . ."

He looked around, dumbfounded, and was about to speak his mind. How is it any of your business how many kids I have? I'm the kind of person who won't be satisfied until I have at least two more . . . However as he glanced around the room he realized that all of the women were looking at him with the same expression on their faces. Those expressions were all saying one thing. You oblivious fool. Get a grip.

"No, no. I have to have more."

Among the women there was even one who sat up straight with a clenched fist. The nurse came in closer.

"Hurry up! We don't have all day!"

"I said I can't."

He unconsciously took a step back, but he was surrounded by women on all sides. For the last time, the nurse pushed the form under his nose. He was near tears as he gave it one last protest, "This can't happen . . ." as he looked at the nurse, the old woman, his mother-in-law and the other women.

"Hurry up and do it!"

"What kind of man is so indecisive?'"

"He already has two. What more does he want?"

"He has no idea what his wife is going through. No wonder he's being berated."

The murmuring, shouting, whispering and bad-mouthing all attacked him at once. "I'll do it. I'll do it, okay?" he mumbled, looking ready to cry.

From that day forward, he found himself leashed. Short-leashed by his wife.

FIGHTING!

HAVE YOU EVER heard of Goalball? Three players on each team take turns rolling the ball toward their opponent's goal, which are like the end zones in American football. The ball is about as big as a basketball, but it seems quite heavy. Defense is played by throwing oneself down like a goalkeeper or even like a bowling pin, for the block when the ball rolls toward the players. There are even rules for things such as penalty kicks. When one occurs, only the player who broke the rule guards the goal. Fortunately, the goal isn't as wide as a soccer field, but instead closer to the size of a volleyball court. Unfortunately, it's too wide to guard alone, so one should be careful not to break any rules. One of the rules players often break is taking off their eye masks. Yes, the players have on eye masks which blindfold them during the game. Fascinating, isn't it? If they're taken off unintentionally, that is, if the eye masks slip off, the referee stops the game and puts them back on the players again. And of course there's a referee. The game has everything. When I once saw it on television, there was even a commentator.

According to the commentator, an expert on Goalball, there were many cases in which the point differential is larger than ten points. However, only rarely in an international game will there be more than a three-point difference in the score. International?

you may ask. Yes, even for this game, which looks as simple as child's play, there were national teams. There were also timeouts. During timeouts, the coach sometimes pressured the players. "Why can't you move a little faster, be stronger, more active?" The players took off their eye masks and quietly took in the coach's hard words as they wiped away beads of sweat.

During the game, the players continuously shouted out "Fighting!" before rolling the ball, after blocking a ball, after scoring a goal, and even after giving up a goal. It wasn't an action-packed game, but the "Fighting, fighting, fighting" numbed your ears. It was loud beyond description. So when I was just about to turn the channel, I heard the following information.

Most of the players were either weak-sighted or have hand-icapped vision. So the eye masks probably completely blocked out any light that's left. To them "fighting" was a signal to one another that meant, "I'm here." It was a confirmation of existence among people who, from a world of limited visibility, had been plunged into a world of perfect darkness. "Fighting, fighting, fighting, fighting!" The longer the game went on, the hoarser the players' voices became.

That was some insight about Goalball, which will bring more involuntary tears to your eyes the more you watch the game, and the audience's voices will become hoarse along with the players' voices.

DR. LONGEVITY

THE VOICE ON the other end of the call didn't seem like an old man's. I asked two more times, thinking it might be Dr. Oh Jang-Soo's assistant, but he said it was him. After all, he's a renowned food and nutrition expert, and a man who writes over two hundred pages while traveling to give lectures more than ten times a month, even though he's past the age of seventy. When I told him the name of the publishing firm I operated, he quickly indicated that he recognized it by asking if it was the one that worked mainly on health-related books. The conversation ran smoothly from there.

"I called you after reading your article in the paper. I wanted to ask you if you were interested in publishing a collection of your columns."

"It's only been a couple of weeks since I started the columns . . . You move very quickly."

"You're a very famous man, doctor. My wife's one of your biggest fans."

Actually, that was a bit of an exaggeration. All she said was, "He looks a lot younger in person than on TV," after she'd seen him at an open lecture in the women's meeting hall at City Hall. At any rate, he told me where to meet him, in a voice that clearly conveyed a satisfied and relaxed tone. When I arrived, I saw that it was a coffee shop bustling with young people all dressed in fancy and flimsy spring fashion.

"Goodness, there are so many young girls here, I feel like a fish out of water. You, Doctor, seem to be very young at heart."

Dr. Oh's eyes became crescent-shaped as he smiled at my babbling, and even his smile was a fabulous one that you'd typically see on a middle-aged man, maybe in his fifties. The old man, despite being seventy years old, had almost no wrinkles, let alone any age spots, and pretty much a full head of hair.

"What would you like?"

A young woman in an ultra miniskirt pressed us for our order. Despite her tone, he took his time looking at the menu. I ordered coffee and he opted for strawberry juice. While we were talking, the girl brought over our juice and coffee and rather than giving him the juice, she placed the juice in front of me and the coffee before him.

"No, over there."

As I asked her to switch the drinks, it was difficult to fathom what Dr. Oh's thoughts were, ordering strawberry juice at his age. He used a straw to noisily slurp the red strawberry juice. Perhaps noticing my stare, he said the following:

"Strawberries are able to suppress the production of nitrosamine, which is a strong carcinogen. If you mash a strawberry into liquid form, you can see that it restricts the growth of viruses. There is also a thing called pectin in strawberries that lowers your cholesterol. I'm guessing that you, Mr. Jung, may also have a bit of high cholesterol."

I'd recently been a little sensitive about my weight, so I made a small rebuttal.

"I might be fat, but my wife is as skinny as a rail. Her cholesterol is lower than average. Our combined number as a couple is similar to others."

"No, that's bad for both of you. You want average. Not low, not high. People hear about cholesterol so often that they get hypersensitive about something like egg yolks, but tell your wife to have egg yolks. Yolks are nutritionally perfect."

"What about this coffee?"

The doctor looked into my eyes and explained things one by one.

"Anything that humans consume has some type of beneficial effect. Coffee isn't as bad as they make it out to be. Caffeine is in coffee. Caffeine promotes brain activity and relaxes the muscles in your bronchial tubes. That means it's good for asthma. It also works as an anti-depressant. Older people who have a hard time maintaining their blood pressure can benefit from having a cup before their meals. There's a substance called tannin in coffee that's actually effective in preventing cavities."

I was in complete admiration on the spot. I agreed to receive the manuscript in six months, and the terms were also relatively generously set, compared to other authors. Whenever I had to call the doctor or meet him, instead of having someone else go, I'd meet him myself because I anticipated receiving counsel about any health problems or concerns that I'd had. That alone would be worth the generous terms of the contract.

Dr. Oh said he wasn't originally the healthy type. Several times since the time he was born, he found himself with serious illnesses that brought him close to death and he was constantly facing minor health issues. This caused him to take an interest in anything health-related early on. As a result, he ended up teaching food and nutrition at a university and since his thirties hadn't had to deal with so much as a cavity or athlete's foot. He was living a happy life, having achieved the three pillars of wealth, honor, and health.

Right before the book was released, I had the opportunity
to visit his house. I needed his personal stamp but since he was
in another part of the country for a lecture, his wife was going
to stamp hers at their home instead. The doctor's house was a
cozy traditional-style house located on a quiet and sunny street
in the neighborhood. You could see the persimmon and jujube
trees from outside the wall fence, and upon entering the gate the
short five-flavored berry and matrimony vine trees formed a nice
ensemble together with the taller trees. These trees were not only
picturesque but their fruits all had much to do with longevity. I'd
gathered enough information from the doctor to roughly recognize the greenery planted in different spots of the yard and their
good effects. Pumpkins, which are good for diuresis; burdock,
which removes toxins from the body; green onions, which make
for a good medicinal treatment of rheumatism; white radishes,
which are good for indigestion; and the lotus root in the pond
could stop any nosebleed. I'd taken it upon myself to make this
trip instead of sending one of my employees in order to check
out what the doctor had planted in his house, and to get some
tips for my own house and diet.

Dr. Oh's wife seemed a little depressed. She had a lot of white
hair and wrinkles like any other seventy-something-year-old
woman. Is this man keeping his secrets to health and longevity
all to himself? I guess he's not doing anything for his wife. Seized
by such thoughts, I was sipping tea when I heard something
shatter from inside the house. Mrs. Oh ran inside and soon I
heard loud voices that sounded like arguing. At last, a flushed
Mrs. Oh emerged and apologized.

"Is there someone inside?"

Mrs. Oh mumbled, "It's my mother-in-law."

"Goodness! May I ask her age?"

"She'll be ninety-six this year. She still has so much energy that she takes it out on her daughter-in-law every day."

Her look told me that she'd pretty much given up, and I couldn't help but think that living a long, healthy life didn't always promise happiness.

A LONELY MAN

AS YOU KNOW, my occupation is writing. It's my opinion that being a writer isn't something you can openly tell others about, as it would be, for instance, for office workers or farmers, especially to someone who interrogatingly asks, "What's your job?" Being a writer isn't a job that's as secretive as being a spy or as amazing as being president or a professional baseball player, but it nonetheless feels like a word that's hard to pronounce when you have to say it with your own lips.

Anyway, I was asked that very question by a fairly old government employee, sitting at a desk with the sign, "Passport Issuance." It seemed that the recent initiative indicating that civil administration was now being provided to help citizens wasn't entirely a joke. The clean and pleasant office had a printer spitting out various documents, computers standing close by, and a long wooden desk that looked like a bar in one of those old western movies, separating civilians from government employees. All this was enough to make someone like me, who visited City Hall twice a year at most, double-check that I was in the right place. The only exception to this was the elderly government employee sitting at the passport issuance window, who gave me a sense of comfort that I was at the right place because he seemed so familiar, oh, that's right, he resembled the government worker I met when I visited the community service center to get my ID card issued for the first time, way back when.

"I said, 'what's your job?'"

When the man in charge of passport issuance asked me the question, I answered, "I make a living writing," in a weak voice that befitted a person who avoided talking about his occupation so much that he couldn't even fill out the job box on a form. He must not have heard me because he straightened his shoulders to ask in a slightly ruffled tone, "What?" I couldn't help but remember the time that I was scolded for bringing a blurry photo for my ID card.

"Says you're a university graduate. Why are you so slow?"

He had already quickly and efficiently taken note of the box asking for my highest level of education, and then reprimanded me for my sluggishness. So I corrected my occupation to "agriculture." I did in fact produce some green onions and peppers in my small vegetable garden, and writers and farmers did have in common that they produce something.

"Why are you changing what you said? Don't you know what your own job is?"

"I'm sorry. Please make it agriculture."

He gave me a once-over and, using a ruler, drew a diagonal line crossing out the box for my job, title of position, office number, etc. I was all of a sudden unemployed, but that I could take.

"What's with your handwriting? This is an official document that'll be typed into a computer."

He provided the free service of closely inspecting every letter that I had scribbled down, being pressed for time because of another appointment, and he proceeded with a precision blade to help up the slanted letters and to scrape the letters that'd dropped out of line. So I had no choice but to swallow his criticism. After all, you could say I was at fault for coming during the short amount of spare time I had before an engagement, to apply for a passport that I had no intention of using for a while, but wanted just because others seemed to have it. Giving me more than enough time both to deeply regret my decision to come and to tell myself, "I'll eat my hat if I ever come for such uselessness again," he slowly but meticulously did everything the way he wanted to, and asked me once again in a stately manner, "Where to?"

"I'm going downtown."

"I'm a busy man, mister, and you keep making jokes. I mean, where are you going with this passport?"

That lousy word "mister" made me hold back one more time, as I hadn't been given such a title in this tough world since I'd been issued my ID card.

"I just want to be prepared."

"Just?"

He shook his head as if he thought I was pitiful and kindly filled in the empty destination box. The country he'd considered appropriate for an unemployed university graduate who had terrible handwriting, and was even unfledged like myself, was Thailand. The purpose of travel? Tourism.

It was like watching a slow-motion video as he cut my photograph to size and glued it on. He proceeded then to take out a slip for the bank deposit and to painstakingly write the amount of the fee for the issuance. I clenched my jaw a couple of times as I patiently waited.

"Go make this deposit now. Do you know where to go?"

When I returned in less than a minute from depositing the money as quickly as Superman himself, he looked a little surprised.

"All done, right?"

He nodded with a look that, for some reason, felt like dejection.

"When will it be ready?"

"In about a week, I guess? Call before you come."

As I spun away from the window as fast as lightning and neared the entrance like a speeding tornado, I could hear his voice calling to me, "Do you know our number? You have to call before you come. It's 533 . . ."

Why was it that his voice felt so sad to me? I turned around and saw that he was looking at me with forlorn eyes as he stood in the low-cast late afternoon sunlight. It was then that I realized that he was lonely. He, too, was a lonely human like I was.

I should've had the sense to get angry at him at a certain point. This darn job that rewards patience as a virtue, and my darn impossible personality. However, I didn't go back to him to ask what the office number was. I wouldn't have any need for the passport for a while, so I wouldn't be returning to get it.

THE PERFECTIONIST

IN MY NEIGHBORHOOD there is a fellow named Dr. Ryu. I have no idea what his area of study is, but his salt and pepper hair, reddish face, and readiness of flowing speech every time he opens his mouth make him look more expert-like than any PhD on the late night discussion programs on TV.

He's also the main goalkeeper for the morning soccer club I'm a part of. Since he was the oldest member of the club, we thought he'd be better suited for a position like goalie, one that didn't require covering much of the field. Though that's the opinion of other players, Dr. Ryu thinks that he's naturally the goalkeeper because he knows more about soccer than anyone else. In soccer, giving up a goal is defeat and scoring a goal is victory, so what position could be more important than goalie? He also insists that he's the only one for the position because the goalkeeper alertly observes the opponents' strengths and weaknesses and devises strategies. He tends to shout "good!" or "bad!" in front of the goal, louder than the coach himself, whether before, during, or after the game. He yells so loudly and nags other players so much throughout the game that everyone else is at a loss of words.

"That fool! Idiot! Blockhead!"

"You call that a header? I could pass better with my butt."

Of course, since there aren't commentators or sportscasters for a friendly match between local clubs, if you go behind the goal where Dr. Ryu stands you can hear the commentary of a sportscaster, coach, player, and cheering section combined into one. The members of the soccer club put up with his criticisms and his nagging because of his various virtues, his age, his unusually loud voice, his extensive knowledge, and strict sense of logic. I don't know, it's probably because, first and foremost, the members of the soccer club are simply nice people.

Simple, nice people aren't only to be found in the soccer club. The members of our community are second-to-none when it comes to kindness and acceptance. Once Dr. Ryu starts roaming about the neighborhood, even the rampant, defiant, and reckless kids from the next town seem to become tame. If they do anything that catches his eye, they'll instantly be in for a reprimand that feels like a thunderclap. And if that doesn't work, they're grabbed by the ears to be taken to their parents. And if that doesn't work, he takes them to the police. And if even that doesn't work, well, they're just written off as being from a godforsaken household (or in his own terms, "lowly bastards"). Of course, nobody reaches the last of these steps. There's no other way but to be good. As long as our kindhearted neighbors tolerate him, he's the uncrowned lord, the unsworn sheriff, the political analyst, the economist, and the one and only linguist in town.

His talent as a linguist is one of the most remarkable, elegant traits of Dr. Ryu, who's not unlike a turkey, a bird known for its various colors and changing forms. He was the one who made angry demands to the district office and had the sign hanging next to the mineral spring fountain, which read "Point four Meeting," corrected to "Point for Meeting." Everybody thought the Chinese characters in the sign, "Let's Care for

(愛好) Nature" would be corrected to the more appropriate "Let's Appreciate (愛護) Nature," but they just ended up becoming "Let's Love Nature" without the Chinese characters. My mistake in always thinking that "placards" were "plangcards" was a minor issue compared to all that. In the entire neighborhood, he was the only one who could distinguish between, explain the differences of, or point out the error of homophones like geenyum as in "commemorate (記念)" or geenyum as in "pray (祈念)," geeneung as in "function (機能)" and geeneung as in "skill (技能)," and sungboon as in "element (成分)" and sungboon as in "character (性分)."

The misspelled words on menus in local food spots, for example, "stirr-fried squid -> stir-fried squid," "spicy sause rice sticks -> spicy sauce rice sticks," "kimchi stu -> kimchi stew," and "spicy beep soup -> spicy beef soup," were pointed out every time he visited the restaurant so that people had no choice but to correct them. He even corrected the signs in the most obscure corners of the neighborhood, like "Ise -> Ice" and "Seling -> Selling" with his relentless nagging. I don't know how he ended up in a hair salon but there's no doubt that the change from "stress perm" to "straight perm" was his doing.

For all that, I consider people like Dr. Ryu to be the salt of the earth, though I never flattered him in that way personally. He was a perfectionist. The "-ist" part of the word indicates that one strives for the concept. It doesn't guarantee perfection but means that one's on the journey to attain it. Perhaps it's the fact that he sometimes forgets the meaning of "-ist" in "perfectionist" which reflects his character as a "perfectionist." He'd truly become a perfect being if he'd only realize this, and that's what I worry about. A perfect human being is no longer human because such a being can't play or live among us, and I don't want to see him go away. So I've saved an anecdote regarding his imperfect side for myself.

I remember that rain had started to sprinkle on the afternoon
of that day. As evening fell, the rain subsided and that's when
he leisurely strolled into my store in an old pair of sweatpants.

"Hey, manager, busy day, huh?"

It'd been less than a year since I opened my small corner food
store, and I wasn't used to being called "manager."

"Yes, it's the rain, Dr. Ryu."

He naturally accepted the title of doctor as if he were born
with it. It was no different from how a real doctor would feel
about the title.

"Do you think you could give me a bottle of beer?"

"Beer?"

"Yeah, the day's making me feel like having a drink. But I
don't have any money on me, and I feel strange about starting
a tab . . ."

My tension was gone. As such, he was perfect. He'd only have
a free drink after making sure that it was indeed free. As a fan,
I gladly gave him the answer he was hoping for.

"Of course, I'd be glad to give you a bottle or two. Is something up?" I asked as I opened the bottle.

He replied nonchalantly, eyes fixed on the television screen,
"Is that the, uh, drama show where the village chairman char-
acter isn't on anymore because the actor's running for National
Assembly?"

"Yes, you're talking about Choi Bool-Am. I heard he didn't
make the vote."

"My mother's curious about it. She's been a fan of *Eventide
Smoke* for a decade. And she's been asking where the village
chairman went."

"I see."

"My mother's ninety and even now it's her sole joy to watch

Eventide Smoke."

"Yes, but nowadays it's not easy to catch sight of evening smoke coming out of people's homes when they cook dinner."

"Not the real smoke, *Eventide Smoke.*"

"I don't know. *Smoke* is better viewed around evening time. Are you saying there's fake smoke? I wonder if you mean briquette fire . . . I'm confused."

"I rarely watch TV so I'm not sure when *Eventide Smoke* is on. Anyway, mother . . ."

"Oh, so you're talking about *Countryside Story.*"

"Hmm. *Eventide Smoke.* Your pronunciation is really bad."

I hid my smile. A ninety-year-old person could've confused *Countryside Story* for *Eventide Smoke.* Actually, I thought *Eventide Smoke* was a more endearing title for the program. The highlight of his visit came when he was stumbling toward the door of the store after scoring one free bottle of beer and a small bottle of drinkable yogurt for his mother.

"Give me a strawng if you have one."

I obediently took out a straw and handed it to him, and as soon as he disappeared and was onto the next block, I let out a loud laugh.

UNDERCOVER

AFTER STARTING THE day in a rush, without even a bite of breakfast, the group had only just reached the top of the hill around lunchtime. They stopped the car as soon as a sign for a restaurant appeared. In front of the restaurant was a parking lot that was so humongous it looked insatiable, and in it were large vehicles like tank trucks and bulk trucks, and even a dust-covered sedan or two.

"The 00 Buckwheat Noodle Garden was featured on the national program *Taste and Style Showcase*. We serve all our customers with side dishes and entrees made with the best green vegetables in the country and mineral water produced from 00 Mountain."

This was what was written on the banner hanging in front of the restaurant.

"Why are you still reading that?" asked the oldest of the group, Kim, tapping me.

"I don't know, I'm confused if that makes sense."

"Well, you can ask the owner. What's important is that they prepare food well. I'm famished."

In the restaurant we found quite a number of people leaning toward their bowls and shoveling food into their mouths. As soon as our group was seated, a woman in tight clothes came around with heavy-set blue-hued porcelain cups and a jug of water.

"You can place your order."

Kim always had questions for all the women he met on the road. He of course had a question for this woman.

"Are you the owner?"

She looked too young and brash to be the owner. At the same time, her clothes and appearance were, to put it nicely, eclectic, and to put it bluntly, loud. Probably no owner would approve of an employee dressing that way.

"Why do you ask?" she asked, slightly raising her eyes. It seemed she didn't want to answer with a simple yes or no.

"It's just that my friend wanted to know," Kim said, pointing at me with his chin. However, I'd lost interest at that point. Since when was cable TV nationally televised? Is there even a program called *Taste and Style Showcase*? Who got to decide on the best wild vegetables and mineral water in the land, and when and how did they do it? Such questions can only be asked when your stomach isn't growling and is more relaxed, and when the person sitting across from you looks like the best restaurant owner in the land.

"No, I'm good. I'm not curious."

When I shook my head, her eyes became sullen. I worried that I might seem like a hooligan going around harassing younger women, so I hurriedly changed the subject to ordering. The problem was that all five of us wanted something different. Bibimbap, broth with short ribs, beef stew, buckwheat noodles, and bean paste stew.

"Come on, that's too complicated. Let's unify, you know, try to order fewer dishes."

I wasn't sure if I had anything to be sorry for, but in light of what'd just happened, I made the suggestion. A member of the group refuted it, however.

"It's not the national communist convention. We're all hungry, you know. We each have the right to eat what we think is delicious."

"I've been waiting for three days. I'm not giving up my bean paste stew."

"No, we can't not eat buckwheat noodles at a house that is famous for buckwheat noodles. I'm not giving that up, either."

For a second, she impassively seemed to watch our squabble before she interrupted with, "No buckwheat noodles."

"What are you talking about? No buckwheat noodles at a buckwheat noodle restaurant?"

"Mister, it's autumn. Nobody eats buckwheat noodles in autumn."

As she was trying to teach Kim, who prided himself on being the country's biggest fan of buckwheat noodles, she turned her head to see if anyone was coming in. Kim was an impatient man and got miffed.

"Then why do you still have that sign? It says buckwheat noodles as big as your front door, and you don't serve buckwheat noodles? That's like animal crackers without any of the animals!"

"Yeah, like walnut pastries without the walnut filling. I'm hungry already, let's unify our choices! Who wants bean paste stew?"

"I don't want to unify."

"Man, you're saying some dangerous things in violation of national policy. Don't forget how close we are to the ceasefire line. Spicy beef soup, anybody?"

"I don't like spicy beef soup. It's too fatty."

"The spicy beef soup isn't fatty."

She tried to enlighten a man who had spicy beef soup for breakfast for the past three days.

"Then let's make it three bean paste stews and two spicy beef soups. There."

One of us put an end to the discussion, preventing the rest from saying anything else. When she got the order, she yelled "Three bean pastes and two spicy beefs!" toward the kitchen and approached a fellow in his fifties who'd just walked through the door. The fellow took a quick look around and was about to turn away saying, "We're in a hurry." Thanks to that, the restaurant patrons felt like they were in the way of the urgent business of this person in a hurry. The woman handled the guy with the savvy of someone who'd dealt with countless people in a hurry.

"Everything's quick. How many are in your party?"

"Four."

"You could have the spicy beef soup. It's the quickest."

"Sure."

Damn, if we'd known that she'd be so obliging, we would've talked to her abruptly too. While we were grumbling, the fellow in his fifties shouted to his party outside, and soon his group slowly walked in and took their seats. While pouring water into bottles for that group, she dropped the cap, and of all places, the cap rolled all the way to my feet. When I reached down to pick it up, I noticed there were food crumbs all over the floor. She nearly snatched the cap out of my hand and used the rag on the next table to wipe off the red sauce smudged on it. Not giving a damn whether the drinking water would flow over the spot that was wiped with the dirty rag, she quickly filled the bottle and went to the other table that was in a hurry. Before anyone could say anything, they hurriedly took the bottles to their mouths. My jaw dropped open at first, but I guess it was understandable if people were in a hurry.

The really funny thing happened after that. Food was served to the group that was in a hurry before we were served.

"Hey, auntie! Get over here!"

The other group of guys were shoveling the spicy beef soup into their mouths, even before my friend who hated spicy beef soup called to the woman, who for sure wouldn't like the word auntie, and began to complain. As I watched the spoons filled with red broth go in and out of their mouths, I couldn't help but be reminded of the kimchi sauce that'd smudged the water bottle cap, and I instantly lost my appetite.

"Why are you serving them before us?"

Standing in front of me, she looked down at me as if dealing with a whining child. That prompted in me a feeling that I hurry up and say what I wanted to say.

"I'm not going to have spicy beef soup. I'm going to have the bibimbap as originally planned."

She slightly raised her eyebrow.

"You can't change your order now."

"Why not? You people are the ones who disregarded our orders in the first place. This wouldn't have happened if you'd served us in the proper order."

However, she wasn't listening to me. She'd already turned her body toward the kitchen and yelled something in an annoyed tone. That was all it took to bring out all the pettiness bubbling below the surface.

"Old lady! Why won't you listen? I'm not having anything other than bibimbap!"

"Mister, I won't charge you for your bowl of spicy beef soup, so you can eat it or not eat it if you don't want to."

"This isn't about the spicy beef soup. Why don't you treat a person with respect? I'm going to have bibimbap, and I want it quickly like they got their spicy beef soup."

The others who were amusedly watching the exchange between the woman and myself all started mumbling at once.

"I'll have the buckwheat noodles," "I'll have the short rib soup," "I want unification . . ."

"I can't take all this. Forget it, we're not selling food to you. No."

I can't recall who took the hand of the woman as she turned on her heels with her rag. Was it me? Or was it Kim?

"Old lady, restaurant permits aren't given to you to serve or not serve customers as you please. Restaurants have a responsibility to provide service to customers who want a meal. If you're open for business, you don't get to decide whether you want to provide this service or not. Listen to me. If I decided to report you to the county office, the people who work here are going to have a difficult time and it'll be a hassle for me, too. But if you insist on not serving us food, I'll go report the restaurant."

A twitch passed through her lips as quickly as a bullet train, and at some point a smile appeared.

"Are you from the provincial office? Or the Ministry of Health and Welfare?"

Surprised, I looked at my group, who now appeared run-down from hunger.

"No."

"Well, why didn't you just say you were from the office? We'll make this right. I'm sorry. What were the dishes you wanted? One bean paste stew, one spicy beef soup, bibimbap . . ."

"I said we're not from the office!"

She stubbornly persisted that we were government workers or something like that who were out for an undercover inspection, saying that only they could make that kind of argument. And she brought us the things that we wanted with lightning speed.

TO "EHY"

IT WAS A gathering of friends, near the end of the year. Now, since people look different, live differently, and talk differently, it's natural that they also observe time differently. There's the one who comes earlier, the one who comes right on time, the guy who starts off early enough, but something always happens on the way so that he ends up being late anyway, and the dude who leaves late but is always luckily on time . . . Counting myself, who's generally late but on time about twice a year, there were five of us. The dude who always left home late and always arrived late still wasn't there.

While waiting for our friend, we started to talk about one thing after another, but it was all about how tough and daunting living in this world was. Tough because of the recession, tough because you feel guilty about your kids when making a deposit into your pension fund, tough to find parking, and tough to take a detour because you don't want to pay the toll using the tunnel. Daunting because you worry that the television dramas will provoke your wife to have an affair, daunting because your junior colleague could make strides and put you on the early retirement list, daunting because of the price hike on leases in the new cities, despite people talking about wanting to live in the garden suburbs. Even after we'd talked about all that, the dude still wasn't there. Drinking the water in the bottle labeled "natural spring water," which was undoubtedly tap water, we continued to have in-depth discussions about the issue of trash, stock market plunges, and the trade balance. The guy was still nowhere to be seen. We were now sick of waiting and a bit mad, so we heatedly exchanged our opinions on North Korean refugees, issues of the Korean Chinese in the Yanbian area, and the invasion of the submarine and how the aftermath took place. All of that came to an end and the bastard still hadn't shown up, not even his shadow.

"Do you want to go ahead and order?"

"No, let's wait just a little longer. He's late but he always comes. We already waited this long."

We didn't want the time we'd spent waiting to go to waste so we agreed to wait a little longer. Accordingly, we had to exchange our views on higher-level issues, or rather hopes. What the next president should be like, the importance of skiing and golf as relaxation activities in a $10,000-GNP era . . . still, we couldn't hear his footsteps. We tried to search for more things to discuss but only confirmed that we were angry. We couldn't find any more common topics to talk about.

"This is too much."

"This is typical of him."

"Do we have to wait longer?"

"I don't see why."

We unanimously decided that we didn't have to wait any longer and ordered. It was thirty minutes past the time we'd promised to meet, and the only reason we lasted this long was that we had more things to talk about than usual, it being the end of the year. As we ordered our food and the dishes started being served, we each let out the complaints we'd been holding back.

"Why is the dude always late? Does he think he's the only one running a business?"

"Does he think he's the only one busy at the end of the year?"

"Does he think he's the only one who's his own boss?"

"Does he think he's the only one getting around by car?"

"Does he think he's the only one who's busy? Ehy?"

When the last one to roast our friend added an awkward "ehy," our withering conversation picked up a second life. According to him, our friend who was always late had the habit of adding the interjection "ehy" to emphasize everything he said. Adding that the interjection was the byproduct of a time when people wouldn't listen to other people, he added a quiet "ehy" at the end. One of the guys presented the opinion that the interjection originated from "eung" which comes from "Isn't that right, eung?" "Eung" is a type of baby talk that's used to insist on something either when one's not convinced of what one's saying or to seem cute. The friend who strongly advocated this opinion slyly added in an "ehy" at the end, which received unspoken admiration from the rest of us. Dishes were served alongside the drinks. However, we were already too far into the discussion to be calmed down by the customary food and drink routine.

"Hey, doesn't the red pepper powder in the bean sprout salad look especially exotic today, ehy?"

"You just said that to use 'ehy' in a sentence, didn't you, ehy?"

"When did I say 'ehy,' ehy?"

"You just said 'ehy,' ehy?"

"You don't want me to say 'ehy' so that you can be the only one saying 'ehy,' ehy?"

"Man, please stop saying 'ehy.' I'm getting a headache, ehy."

"Anybody who says 'ehy' from this point forward is paying, ehy?"

"You just said 'ehy,' aight? You can pay for everything, aight?"

"Enough with the 'aights' or 'ehys,' eez . . ."

I suddenly wondered if our friend was sacrificing himself by running late on purpose to provide us the opportunity to have this pure moment of childlike joy and bonding through laughter. I wondered if he was smiling to himself as he watched us. However, being a part of this group of friends, he wasn't the type to be late by design or as a part of such a deeply thought-out, diabolical plan. And just then he arrived, slipping into our booth, naturally late because he'd left his house late, and, as always, unapologetic and dignified as a prince. However, when he showed up none of us gave heed to his entrance, as we were busy wreaking havoc with the "ehys" and wagging our fingers at one another. That is, before he set down his heavyset build and waved his hand around to get our attention, and then said something from his heart, in a slow and unwavering voice.

"Enough chitchat! Gentlemen, the year is coming to an end, bringing with it a new year. Let us forget about all that's happened this past year and have a great new year . . ."

He picked up his glass, and we watched intently as he let out the exclamation we'd all been waiting for, with such ease.

"Ehy?"

His naturally flowing "ehy" was neither heavy nor light, neither long nor short, neither cheap nor boisterous, and being left speechless and mesmerized, we couldn't help raising our glasses high. "Cheers, ehy!"

THE RED ROSE HANDKERCHIEF

PROFESSOR RYU WAS always clad in a suit, with a crisp white shirt and bow tie. He always passed through campus at the same exact time, with a shiny leather bag by his side. Though there was some white in his hair, he still had a youthful head of hair, and his face was flushed like a boy's. People wouldn't call him handsome, but they all agreed that he was stylish. But those kind of stylish men were a dime a dozen. In the university alone, there was a star professor who often appeared on television, and also a professor who had a large fan following thanks to a book of his essays. They were all also stylish. Professor Ryu was only committed to his lectures and didn't do anything else. However, he was the most popular professor on campus.

He didn't care for lectures that were easy for students to digest, he never exerted extra effort to entertain students, and he made students earn their grades. However, whoever attended his signature lecture, which was an annual event, couldn't help but like him. It'd be more precise to say people would not only like him, but they'd find themselves in awe and come to love him.

His slightly altered attire indicated when it was time for the special annual lecture. The black suit, black shoes, black socks, white dress shirt, and black bow tie remained the same, but a red handkerchief was tucked into his upper suit pocket. When he entered the campus gates with that red handkerchief in his chest pocket, word spread like a wave to the far corners of the university. Most classes in the same time slot as his lecture, including the ones by the other stylish professors, might as well have been cancelled. Professors who were his junior colleagues or former students often canceled their own classes if they were in the same time slot. Some of them attended Professor Ryu's lecture themselves, just to sit among students and reminisce about the time when they'd listened to the lecture when they were young. When the time came, when finally the lecture began, the lecture hall became packed, up through the aisles and to the back of the room. Even the halls became filled with eager students with the burning desire to learn. In other words, it was the event of the year.

Be that as it may, he always stepped into the hall with the same gait, the same expression, and the same clothes he always wore. He ignored the fact that there was more than twice the normal number of students. He opened his bag and took out his lecture book exactly the way he did in every class. He put his finger on the part where he'd left off last time, and double-checked with the student sitting in the front row. Even this part was the same as usual. In a low voice, he read the title of the part to be read during that day's lecture, and turned his back to write the title on the chalkboard. Although it was the same lecture he'd been giving for decades, he was as prudent as if it were his first time.

What was the title of the passage he was to read, no, had been reading? I regret that it escapes me. Let's just say it was "My Darling Clementine."

Originally, "My Darling Clementine" was sung by the Forty-niners during the age of the western pioneers in America. Forty-niners were people who migrated to the mines of California in America, with the dream of digging up a fortune in the California Gold Rush. In the ten years between 1849 and 1858, these people excavated five hundred and fifty million dollars worth of gold from the Californian mines. It was an enormous amount of money for the times, but not all of the Forty-niners became rich, and most of them suffered from harsh working conditions and hunger. There were many who were dying from accidents, illnesses, and Native American aggression. They came to realize that their gold was filling the pockets of capitalists in New York and San Francisco, and it was around then that a self-deprecating tune entitled "My Darling Clementine" started becoming popular.

There was a miner who dug for gold in a cavern, in the canyon, a Forty-niner. He had a daughter named Clementine. The passage Dr. Ryu was about to read that day began as such.

He read line by line in a clear, high-pitched voice. He chanted on about Clementine's beauty, charm, and the poor life of the Forty-niner. Clementine, so fairy-like. Clementine with her ruby-red lips. The smile in her father's eyes looking at Clementine. Clementine running toward her father. The waves rushing to the shores and endlessly breaking, like the passage of time itself, some white and some drearily blue. But Clementine has now left her poor father forever. One day, Clementine is swept away by a wandering splinter in the water. She falls into the foaming brine, and blows bubbles soft and fine with her ruby lips above the water. However, her father can't swim. So it goes, and so it goes . . .

Professor Ryu's voice became lower and lower, and it began to tremble. His face became crushed with sadness and his shoulders slumped down, down. Everybody held their breath and observed his every move.

"Oh my darling, oh my darling, oh my darling Clementine. You are lost and gone forever. Dreadful sorry, Clementine."

At the very climax of the verse, his sorrowful voice, full of echo, stopped with a halt. He returned to the podium and slowly put his book down. He took off his glasses with his left hand. He lifted his right hand toward the red handkerchief tucked into his breast pocket. Tears flowed from his eyes! These tears have flowed every year, during the same lecture, but they always ran down his cheek with such grief, as if it were the very first time. Those who watched these tears became paralyzed.

He finally took out his red handkerchief with the most graceful tug. A fanciful rose adorns the cloth. Fingers holding the petals of the rose, he stood still and looked out the window. Once in a while, his Adam's apple moved up and down, perhaps in an effort to hold back tears. In the end, he wiped his tears. He wiped his glasses and blew his nose with a blare. There was a strange shrill at the end. Still, no one was laughing. He put his glasses back on and put the handkerchief in his pocket. He slowly picked up his book. He began reading the last part in a calm tone.

"Clementine left, and the miner soon began to peak and pine. In the church yard, in the canyon grew flowers and became vines. Roses blossomed among other posies. Roses fertilized by Clementine . . ."

At exactly the moment he finished reading and closed his book, the bell rang, indicating the end of class. He put the book inside his bag. He took a blank look around the class where nobody dared to get up before the other students, and walked out with the same gait as always. When he entered the hallway, students parted on each side of the hall to make way. The sweep of emotion produced from the lecture has always been shown through a silent awe for decades. He hated applause or cheering and never anticipated or received it.

Once in his room, he'll put down his bag. He'll take out his handkerchief and put it in a drawer which will allow him to leave his room with the same attire he has on every day. He'll realize it's lunchtime when he looks at his watch. He'll take out his handkerchief once again from the drawer. He'll put it in the pocket of his pants, not his jacket, and leave the room. He'll walk to the faculty cafeteria and scrutinize the day's menu. It'd be nice if the menu included braised short ribs. He'll set down his hearty helping of braised short ribs on the table and begin eating. He'll probably be famished after giving the signature lecture of the year. By the time he goes through his second plate of ribs, beads of sweat will form on his nose and forehead. That's when he'll take out the handkerchief from his pocket. He'll repeatedly wipe his sweat with the part of the handkerchief that doesn't have the rose on it. After all, that's why he chose this red handkerchief with a rose.

THE AMUSING LIFE - 2
On Bribing

THERE ARE TWO extraordinary types of humans in this world: people who provide bribes and people who receive bribes. Most people live their lives not having to think about bribes. Most people don't understand why bribes are necessary. Yet the extraordinary humans who have much to do with bribes won't leave the majority of people who have nothing to do with bribes alone. Why? Like I said, they're extraordinary.

These extraordinary people, well, they even drive when they're drunk. It wouldn't be as big a problem if they only drove their own cars (actually, even that's a problem. At best, they would have to be driving alone and be the only one who gets killed), but they try to drive other people's lives. Let me give you an example. About ten years ago, I'd just arrived from the backwoods and went to see my friend to ask him to help me find a room where I could stay. I didn't have the faintest idea that my friend was one of those extraordinary people involved with bribes. My friend suggested that since it'd been a long time, before we went room searching we should catch up and have a drink. He said that having a great drink would help us find a great room. A great room leads to a great job, a great job leads to a great life, a great life leads to a one-way ticket to heaven,

which is said to be so great, and so a great room is practically
the first step to heaven, right? The bar was a joint that my friend
frequented for his bribe-related business. As we got ready to leave
at around midnight, we looked at the bill, which was as fancy as
the face of the woman who owned the bar. Until then, at least,
I'd had nothing to do with bribes, so I didn't do anything stupid like pay the bill with what was to be my future rent money.
That seemed to come as a surprise to my friend. He dawdled as
he asked to put the bill on his tab, and glanced at me before he
started his car and steered onto the road. I asked the question I
had on my mind, in an honest yet discreet manner.

"Is it okay to drink and drive in Seoul nowadays?"

"Hey, hillbilly! My house isn't even far enough for you to be
babbling about driving under the influence or not driving under
the non-influence. I know this neighborhood like the sole of my
foot. Why don't you just stay crumpled up right where you are?"

I retreated back into my seat and decided to trust my friend,
who came to Seoul and got settled early on. The owner of the bar
was sitting in the passenger seat, as she'd been promised that she'd
get a ride home if she let my friend run a tab. She said that she
lived in the same neighborhood as my friend. Anyway, we were
less than a couple of kilometers along when an "eeeoooeeeooo"
with great flashing lights seemed to grab us by the back of our
necks, and a motorcycle blocked us off.

"Oh, no, we're in trouble."

In my mind, this was a catastrophe. I had my friend buy me
drinks, drive me in his car, and now I was about to see him get
caught driving under the influence. But my friend was calm. He
stopped the car, turned on the interior lights and rolled down
the window. He greeted the man with an energetic flair.

"Hello, officer!"

The man who got off the motorcycle wore a helmet like an astronaut and a uniform like a policeman. Seeing how he wore sunglasses even though it was dark, I thought he might've had a passion for sunglasses. The police officer seemed apathetic toward the world, raising his hand in a half-hearted salute. "We're checking for DUIs," he said lethargically. "Can you please breathe into this?"

The policeman pushed a paper cup forward and my friend shook his head.

"I didn't drink."

The policeman yawned as if to say I'm tired of seeing so many guys like you, and lazily opened his mouth once more.

"Hah! I took the trouble of following you since you left the bar. Now, come on."

My friend hastily glanced around to see if anyone was around as he replied, "I work there."

"That's right, sir. Why don't you come by sometime?" asked the bar owner in the passenger seat, trying to pitch in.

"I guess talking to you in a friendly way isn't going to work."

Did the cop ever talk in a friendly way? Anyway, he took from his waist a breathalyzer that had a straw on it and pointed it at us inside the car like a pistol. Finally, my friend waved his hand in protest and started coming up with excuses.

"Please sir, cut me some slack. My house is right inside that alley. I live in the neighborhood."

"I must ask you to blow."

"How can I blow on something so disgusting? I'll never put something in my mouth that's touched the lips of someone else."

All the while that he was doing this, my friend was frantically waving his other hand at me. What do you want me to do? In my wallet, I had a check and several hundred thousand won that I was going to use to pay for a room. It was money stained with the tears and snot of my beloved mother, who lived alone and had tucked the money in my wallet so I could get started with my success in Seoul. Was it this money my friend was waving for? How much of it? I couldn't think straight.

"This is a new straw. If you still think it's dirty, I'll gladly change it for you, man."

At that point, the cop was talking quite casually, as if to a friend. I remained balky when my friend shook his fingers toward me, and he snapped his fingers in a threatening way. The sternness of the sound made me take my wallet out of my pocket before I knew it and I handed it over to my friend.

"Fine, my good friend. How much will it take?"

"What do you think you're doing? Do you take me for some kind of bargainer?"

"Hey, I know how hard it is to work out here in the cold. I'd like you to go get a bowl of stew or something."

As he talked, my friend took all but the check from my wallet, and with deft hands pushed it toward the cop. The cop pocketed the money in a dazzling sweep and said, "How can you be driving like this when police are everywhere these days? I'm going to let you go since you say you live close by, but you should be careful. Do you want me to escort you?"

"Forget it, forget it. I live right there. Damn, just my luck."

Actually, it was just my luck. My hands were trembling as I took back my now skinny wallet. I pictured my mother all alone, out in the countryside. Mother, look at me, barely through my first day in Seoul . . . But my friend still wasn't through with the cop.

"Hey, officer, give me that for a second. I paid good money, I should at least have a blow at it."

"I thought you said it was dirty? Come on, let's go."

I stopped in the middle of my lamenting to prompt my friend to go home, but he didn't budge.

"How can I go without trying a machine that costs you several hundred thousand won for a single blow?"

He took the straw the cop pushed toward him and blew hard. The cop smirked as he looked at the screen, and let out a "huh." The number showed 0.00.

"That's strange."

The cop rotated the straw and offered it to my friend again. Once more, my friend blew into the straw all of the alcohol particles included in the dozens of bottles of beer we'd consumed that evening. However, the number was still 0.00. We didn't know what was going on, but all of us, especially me, were bursting with annoyance. The policeman apologized, saying that the machine seemed to be broken, though that didn't bring back the money that'd already gone in his pocket.

"I'll escort you to your house. Follow me."

"Lay off!"

I was suddenly talking to the cop casually, too. That was the first time I got a glimpse of the extraordinary people in the industry of bribery.

Time passed and I not only found a room, but also a job. I don't know if my friend's business prospered or not during this time, but it turned out that he could, alas, no longer enjoy his hobby of driving under the influence. A normal policeman, who didn't know how to exchange bribes, stopped my friend with a blood alcohol level that would've made an elephant drunk. My friend made sure to check if he was, by any chance, an extraordinary human of the bribery industry, and if he wasn't, whether he'd be interested in joining. But he happened to be a policeman who did his job honestly, so bribery didn't work. He was lucky not to be arrested. He paid a fine amounting to five times what he'd offered as his bribe, and his license was revoked. After that, he got in touch with me. It was the first time we'd met since the incident.

My friend brought his car to the place where we met. His new hobby appeared to be driving without a license. When you think about it, driving under the influence and driving without a license have a lot in common in that they both give you a thrill, and both are harmful except for one sole benefit, which is that you have to strictly observe all driving regulations so that you won't get pulled over. As soon as he spotted me, my friend ushered me into his car. As he drove, he told me we should have a cup of tea in his office, that he didn't drink these days, that there was no fun in driving drunk since he no longer had a license to be taken away. He also told me the heroic tale of how he became a giant in the world of bribery, during the time since we'd last met. We'd almost made it to his office when we were stopped at a traffic light and I was allowed to witness an entirely different side of the world of bribery.

As the car stopped, my friend opened the window for a smoke. That's when he locked eyes with the policeman sitting in the passenger seat of a patrol car in the next lane. As soon as their eyes met, my friend looked away to my side. But they aren't called policemen for nothing. Sensing something was strange, the policeman signaled to us to pull over to the side. We didn't have time to switch seats, and it's not like I had time to think of handing my friend my own driver's license.

"What's the problem?" my friend asked with his head out the window, stopping the car. The policeman stepped out of his car and approached us, looking completely apathetic toward the world. I guess he had a thing for looking at the glaring sun with his bare eyes in the middle of summer, because he didn't have his shades on. He gave us a half-hearted salute out of formality and asked to see a license.

"Wait, why? Did I do something wrong?"

The policeman replied in a lazy, disinterested tone.

"Why'd you look away?"

I could see the wheels spinning in my friend's head.

"Since when is that a crime?"

"So you admit that you did look away. OK, put it right here, your license."

You could tell from his talk alone that he was a rare species among the police force, one that had an intimate relationship with bribes, an especially adept, seasoned policeman. Even I could tell, so there was no way that my friend, who was not only canny at offering bribes, but also boastful of his keen experience, didn't recognize the type.

"My goodness, is it hot. I want to help you get yourselves some ice cream somewhere. Let off some of that heat."

My friend took out his wallet and while pretending to reach for his license, put on a baffled look and shook his head. It wasn't that he was trying to act like his preciously tucked away license had disappeared in front of the policeman. He didn't see any cash. After a moment to ponder this, my friend gave up and shook his head, took out a check. He waved the check and continued to talk.

"This is all I have on me, and I don't want to ask for change . . . My office is right up there. Do you see that building?"

That was the moment, the moment when the creepy, low voice that could only come from the deep recesses of the throat of a major player in the world of bribery flowed out of the policeman's annoyed face.

"Are you kidding me? Have you ever seen us run a tab?"

"Damn, then. Fine. I'll give you this, just let me off this once."

They didn't elaborate any further. The check that was in my friend's hand swiftly moved to the policeman's hand, and then in the blink of an eye, into the policeman's inner pocket. If I hadn't seen it up close, I wouldn't even have known there'd been an exchange. It was practically an art form.

"My policeman friend, I feel like I've seen your skills somewhere before . . ."

My friend had already taken on a different tone, as if he were talking to a friend.

"Don't be silly. Is your office really there? If it's not, I could give you an escort."

The policeman was also speaking with a different tone. It was the tone of a normal policeman, friendlier, more willing to help, and concerned about the well-being of citizens.

"By any chance . . . didn't you ride around on a motorcycle last winter?"

"Hey, are you the fellow who registered 0.00 on the breathalyzer?"

"Yup. That's me. Fate seems to bring us together. Well, then."

The two waved goodbye to each other. And my friend started his car.

"Hey, how can you give him a check? You should've asked me for money."

"It's fine. It's all done."

Despite his friendly wave, my friend seemed quite put out. It was no wonder, since he'd ended up giving several hundred thousand won to that one policeman.

"How much was the check worth?"

"Three hundred and fifty thousand won."

"Wow, the guy really scored big today. I didn't know there were bank checks for three hundred and fifty thousand won."

"It's a personal check."

"Yeah?"

Suddenly my friend broke into a smile.

"I just remembered, it's a bad check."

NONESSENTIAL INFORMATION. In the end, my extraordinary friend became so involved with offering bribes that he neglected his actual business and ended up going bankrupt. In the end, the extraordinary policeman got caught accepting a bribe by another policeman, and was discharged when he tried to bribe his way out of the situation. After that, he was seen driving around selling apples from a truck.

Another piece of nonessential information. As they say in Buddhism, nothing is certain in this world, and you reap what you sow. Let this be a lesson for us not to make ourselves and others miserable with a bounced check.

LOVE IN THE COURSE
OF THREE LIVES

1

"I" AM CURRENTLY in a romantic relationship. xx:x2 AM, 1xth, 1x, in the year 199x. I call my significant other with my cell phone as I walk on a street near Gwanghwamun. I call because I was paged to call back. My significant other answers the phone in Apgujeong-dong. It's a digital cell phone, which is better than the former analog-style phones, but still it's answered long after it begins to ring. My significant other's voice echoes in waves as if he's in an empty room. He complains that my voice sounds like an alien's.

"Are you going to get a new phone again? Did you text me to tell me that?"

Digital cell phones transmit voice signals in eight thousand pieces, and the sound quality isn't as clear as with the PCS-style phones, which break up voice signals into thirteen thousand pieces, my significant other tells me. He tells me that the reason he wants to get a new phone is to be able to "connect" with me easier and faster whenever he wants. And he complains that it's been too long since I've written him a letter. I get off the phone and walk into a cyber café. I log onto the Internet and find my way to the website that has the poems of the poet, Song Okze, whom I've always liked, and download a love poem. Next, I add some vows of love and send it to my significant other's ID. Once it's sent, his cell phone will ring. He has a service that alerts him when an email has arrived.

My significant other will mumble that he doesn't understand why there still isn't a cell phone that immediately connects to a satellite when it's turned on, and take out his notebook which is as heavy as a stone axe, connect it to his phone and then read the email.

I arrive home. I listen to the message he left me on my answering machine after reading the email. I call his home and also leave him a message on his machine.

"I love you. But you know what? How long have we known each other? I wonder if we'll ever see each other before we die of old age . . ."

2

IN MY FORMER life, that is, one hundred and twenty years ago, "I" was sitting under an old zelkova tree. I lost track of how long I'd been siting there. My love didn't come, only wind and clouds.

All of a sudden, a tiny speck of a person appeared at the end of the dark plain. The person wore a bamboo hat that was nearly destroyed. He had a limp and was slowly walking in my direction with all he had, and it seemed like it would take a hundred years. In my heart, I heard the sound of a tree branch breaking off. It had to be him. It was him! I tore off into the field with my arms wide open. He recognized me too, and threw off his hat to run toward me. We ran and ran again as if death were on our heels. The distance between us went from two kilometers to half a kilometer to ten steps. At last, finally, after all, somehow we held each other tightly.

"My lady, I have come. I have missed you."

"My love, why did you not write? I came out here every day for three years to wait and wait again for you."

"There was no person who could deliver my letters. There wasn't even a torch stand where I could relay the thoughts of the great love I have for you in my humble heart. This humble man has walked for three years to come to you, my lady. I am your letter, your courier, and your torch of light. I am also yours, my lady."

"I have no regrets even if I die this moment. I will never part with you again."

"I, too, have no regrets if I die this moment. Let us not be apart for another moment."

And so in each other's arms, the two of us died, from starvation.

3

HOW WILL WE romance in the next life? Will I stand amidst a subtle scent, a mixture of his favorite cologne and his own unique smell, and forsakenly whisper "I love you" to a hologram based on the way he'd looked when he was at his most youthful and handsome on this earth? He, in return, will receive my message and hologram through an interplanetary communication system transmitted through Jupiter, and probably send a newer version that combines tactile sensations, along with a new scent that he acquired during the ten years he worked at a diamond mine on Neptune.

MY BELOVED TRIBE
OF INFORMAL TALKERS

IN THIS WORLD, there's a tribe called the "Tribe of Informal Talkers." Members of this tribe are trained rigorously to talk informally from the time that they're born. I've actually met a child of this tribe who received such training in one of the most remote areas of the world, surrounded by mountains and near a working water mill. This child came to his father to say, "Dad, Mom says it's time for you to eat, my friend," but when he spotted an adult stranger, he inquired with round, curious eyes, "What brings you all the way here, grown-up man?" He was so cute that I lightly tapped his head, and instantly the child's grandmother, mother, father, uncle, and aunt all came out and scolded me in informal terms, saying that I'd made the child less intelligent. The members of this tribe are scattered all over the country, and I'd like to introduce one member that I've met relatively recently.

The workspace I've recently set up and occasionally visit for my writing is in a rural area that's pitch-black and deserted by nine o'clock at night. You rarely see any lights even in the busiest part of town, near the town hall, except for one karaoke bar and a supermarket. It feels like a lonesome town. One time, I parked my car by the road and crossed the road to the store to buy some

beer to shake off this feeling of desolation. My car was gone by
the time I walked out of the store carrying the items the sleepy-
eyed owner had stuffed into a plastic bag in an impossibly slow
manner. Thankfully, I could see the emergency lights of a police
car not too far away. A fellow was sauntering toward the patrol
car, so I urgently called to him.

"Sir! Sir!"

The fellow turned around and spoke in informal terms as
soon as he opened his mouth.

"You're talking to me?"

At this point, I still hadn't figured out he was a member of
the Tribe of Informal Talkers.

"Yes. Have you seen a parked car around here?"

"It's over there."

As I looked toward where he was motioning, I could see that
my car had been moved to the other side of the road. I thought
I must've mistaken where I'd parked, and walked over to the car
to open the door. The door didn't open. After watching me with
his arms crossed, the fellow slowly approached me.

"So, this is your car?"

I told him I thought so. He unexpectedly raised his voice at
me for neglecting my improperly parked car, the keys inside.
Taking out my keys with one hand, he went on to add that if
it weren't for him, my car would've been stolen for sure and
most definitely would've been used in criminal activity, bringing
disruption to the social order. I courteously thanked him for
noticing that my car door was open, worrying that the car might
get stolen, but also getting into the car to park it on the other
side of the road, locking it, and waiting until the owner came
back, all in the short five minutes that I'd spent in the store, and
asked for my keys back. However, he didn't want to hand them
over that easily.

"Your job? Where do you live?"

At last, that familiar feeling came to me. Oh, an informal talker! However, I wanted to be absolutely sure.

"I'm just a local. So accordingly, I live here in town. Who are you? May I ask your name?"

"Why?"

"I have a feeling that you may be related to the people I once saw when I visited a village deep in the mountains. Your name? Your family clan? Your hometown?"

"Are you trying to pull something on a police officer on official duty?"

"Oh, are you an officer? I didn't realize you were because I've never seen an officer not wearing a hat or wearing sandals. Is there a new rule now that officers should hold a toothpick in their mouth when talking to citizens during their on-duty hours?"

He raised his brows.

"Well, look at that. You should be saying thanks but instead you pick a fight?"

"I believe I did thank you already. Or isn't that considered a thank you? I don't think you're hoping for a bribe or anything."

At that, he narrowed his eyes, which were already as narrow as slits, and demanded that I present my driver's license. I asked him to confirm that he was a police officer first. He yelled at me to show him my license, which I responded to by also yelling that I couldn't show him my license if he didn't identify himself. Dumbfounded, he called another police officer, which was exactly the result I was hoping for. The other officer was in full uniform and was carrying a walkie-talkie. He talked to me with proper formality and I handed him my driver's license. He ran a check on my social security number and name with his walkie-talkie and returned my license.

"You're not even that young. Why do you have to be such a kid and so stubborn about things? We're the same age, you know."

The member of the informal tribe had let up a little bit. I later found out that he was a year younger than me. He did look like he was three to four years older than I was. I asked him to give me back my keys if he was done with everything, and he handed them over as if he were sad to see things end.

"Legally speaking, I could give you a ticket, and you wouldn't be able to do anything about it. All I was trying to do was take care of a fellow townsman and then you got all picky with my uniform and the way I talk. Having a car means you have to take care of it properly, too, you know."

I opened my car door, started the engine, and rolled down the window to say goodbye.

"Well, then. On with your duties, man."

He looked back at me, surprised.

"We belong to the same tribe. Let's meet up at the clan gathering or something."

While he continued to look blankly, I sat back in my seat and drove away toward my workspace.

The next day I bumped into him in front of the town hall. When I asked him for directions to the post office, he answered with perfect honorifics. Not wanting to show him any less respect, I greatly thanked him for his assistance, and he even finished with a salute.

We became very good friends after that.

FYI. How to deal with a member of the Tribe of Informal Talkers: 1) If one is also a member of this tribe, talk informally to confirm that the other is of the same bloodline. 2) If one isn't a member of this tribe, always respond with a loud voice. The rivals of the tribe are the "Whoever Has The Louder Voice Wins" tribe.

I DON'T DO THIS CRAP FOR MONEY

IN KOREA IT isn't difficult to see a certain kind of person that's rare in other parts of the world. The name of this kind of person is "I Don't Do This Crap for Money." These people don't live together but are active members spread across all parts of society, so a normal person doesn't have too much difficulty finding them. The name of their clan isn't printed on their forehead, so it may take a little bit of effort to distinguish them from others. Just a little bit, that's all. I'm about to tell you about a person I met who was from this clan.

There was a toll collector at the highway tollgate. She was a woman in her forties or fifties. This was a tollgate where you'd pay nine hundred won flat instead of a toll calculated according to the distance you travelled, and unfortunately I didn't have change. I took a ten-thousand-won bill from my wallet and handed it to the toll collector. Unless you're a god, it takes time to take money out of your wallet, to move the money from your right hand to left hand, to roll down the window and hand over the money. The toll lady must have become impatient or bored. When I handed her the money she looked as if she were ready to give it back, asking, "Don't you have change?" I shook my head and said no, and even for that it took more time than in normal cases because I speak at a slower pace than others. "Why don't you carry change?" the toll lady asked, with the ten-thousand-won bill still in her hand, in a tone that made it hard to tell if she was asking, criticizing, or trying to teach me. The moment I looked at the money, I no longer feared her, because it was mine, and a bit of annoyance swept over me. So I said, "Hurry and give me the change. Cars are waiting behind me." The toll collector acted as if she'd made a great discovery when she said, "If you're so worried about the cars behind you, you shouldn't be so slow. Besides, there are no cars behind you." She started to count the change.

I briefly fell into thought while she took her time counting the change. Does this old lady want to have some fun with me? Is she trying to advise me to better carry out my role in society by learning how to move more quickly? Or is she just bored and joking around? Or . . . as I thought about it, none of these reasons applied. She was a member of the "I Don't Do This Crap for Money" clan. It took time to form my thoughts, so I didn't get the chance to argue with the member of this great clan and get to the bottom of their existence. All I could do was take the money like a mute, and leave with a humiliated red face.

That day, I was able to encounter many members of the "I Don't Do This Crap for Money" clan. An attendant who oversaw a parking lot next to a high-rise building. The owner of a pretty well-known beef bone soup restaurant. A government employee in charge of civil defense training. A waitress at a coffee shop who had no intention of serving anyone who wasn't interested in her appearance. Perhaps they picked that day to demonstrate and let their existence be known, or maybe it was my rotten luck, or maybe I was just worked up over what'd happened that morning.

On the way home, I came to pass through the toll gate on Namsan. Remembering the lesson I'd learned that morning, I put my hand in my pocket as soon as the tollgate came into view.

I was digging around all of my pockets for change because I only had a single thousand-won bill in my wallet, when I suddenly rammed into the car in front of me that'd stopped to pay its toll.

YES, THAT'S RIGHT

IN THE CITY of Samcheok, in Gangwon Province, there's a pavilion called Jookseoroo. Proudly looking down the rocky precipice by the Osipcheon River, which flows across the city, the pavilion has, throughout history, invited many a writer and painter. The plaque written, 海仙遊戲之所, which translates to "a place where the gods of the sea come to play," shows that it remains a popular site visited by countless tourists. The restroom inside the pavilion is old, yet remarkably clean. Yes, that's right. One could even eat their lunch in there.

As usual, there are dozens of tourist buses from Pohang, Youngju, and Yangpyeong. The people stepping down from the bus are usually already a little red in the face, shoulders still full of rhythm. It's apparent there was no shortage of drinks on the bus. As soon as the women finish their quick trips to the restroom, they begin to enjoy dancing in clusters on one side of the courtyard. The music is produced from a large portable cassette player. The music is mostly cha-cha, rumba, go-go, disco, etc., rearranged into traditional trot-style music. However, the dance includes a wide spectrum of unique movements taken from the likes of traditional Korean dance, the jitterbug, blues dancing, and aerobic dance. The one sound that especially echoes in your ear is the bridge "cha-cha-cha," from "la-di-da la-di-da cha-cha-cha!" In unison people poke the air with their hand and shout the bridge, "cha-cha-cha." In that moment, everybody feels as energetic as they were at twenty or thirty years old. Yes, that's right. These are senior citizens who're at least sixty years old.

Their faces are wrinkled from long hours working the fields under the sun. Yes, that's right. The clothes they have on may be suits and traditional hanboks that are crisp and new, but their hands are rough from raking and turning over dirt for so many years. Using song and dance as an excuse, they stagger and let out their stored up sorrow and resentment, which is rumpled up like a tangle of noodles in the nooks of their backs and chests. They shed their bottled up feelings like falling leaves on the courtyard of Jookseoru, the most beautiful site on the east coast of Korea. Yes, that's right. There's a pavilion manager wearing a cap, with a whistle in his mouth, but he just looks on. There's also a large broom in the far corner of the yard to clean away the traces of these visitors once they leave.

It's time to look for the gods at play. The gods have taken their seats on the wooden floors of the pavilion, enjoying some soju and beer. "Ahh, what I'd give to spend a lifetime playing just Baduk or chess." That's the third time one of them says this. Yes, that's right. He looks comparatively young, but his suit looks ragged, unlike the others'. He shouts for the fourth time. "Ahh, what I would give to spend a lifetime just playing Baduk or chess." His youth has gone. The waters of Osipcheon River flow on, frighteningly blue. It flows downward, downward, for tens of thousands of years.

On the guardrail there's a sign that reads, "Danger! Do not lean!" The guardrail is the only thing that separates one from a perilous fall.

"Do you think it's about a hundred meters?"

"Way deeper than a hundred!"

Two old men with crane-like white hair are mesmerized by the cliff. One of them says he was in the airborne troops. The other says he was in the marines.

"So I guess it's deeper than a hundred meters?"

"Not even!"

The two are drunk. More correctly, they can't help but be drunk. It's the top of the Jookseoru, the most beautiful site on this side of the country.

"Couldn't we jump off from here, eh?"

". . ."

"Do you think we'd kick the bucket if we jumped?"

". . ."

"I think we'd croak."

". . ."

"Would you like to bet on it, my friend?"

". . ."

"Come on, buddy."

"Bet what?"

"An extra large bottle of soju."

"OK, but who will jump?"

"Ahem, you know, I'd jump in a blink if I were only ten years younger."

Finishing their daily discussion, they look down at the winding river, their white hair blowing in the wind. They see a man and woman washing their motorcycle on the other side of the river. Yes, that's right.

Yes, that's right. Yes, indeed. Like a tune that drifts away on passing waters, they, too, drift away. Let's play and enjoy life when we're young. Yes, that's right. Ah, yes, come to think about it, it really is.

HOW OLD ARE YOU?

LIKE THE LINE from that poem that goes, "From even the wind rustling the leaves I have suffered," so was he sensitive to everything around him, down to the titles everyone was given at work. A world that uses social rank as a standard to measure the weight of a person's character is vulgar. However, for him, things became problematic because of the fruitless time he'd invested studying for a national qualification exam for high government official positions that'd grant him a shortcut into high society. His failure to pass relegated him to the life of a regular company employee who had a later start in his career than those in his age group. Naturally, his promotions came later, and now just shy of forty, as the oldest junior manager in the office, and as someone who'd started to worry about his retirement pension plan, the workplace just wouldn't be any fun for him if it weren't for the fun he poked, for no reason at all, at either the newbies in the office or senior-ranking workers who were younger than him.

When the office went out for drinks after work, he'd talk to his senior coworkers very casually, embarrassing those who actually tried to respectfully honor the few years he had on them. He always said that people who wished to call others with the extra "Mr." or "Mrs." or be addressed as such, in order to imply a higher position, had a disgusting tendency to bow to those in power and reign over those who were weak. Nonetheless, it was true that he treated new office workers like his own servants, and also that he treated workers of the same rank as little brothers or sisters.

He'd just arrived at work, and was enjoying the warmth of a paper cup filled with fresh, cheap coffee from the vending machine, when he received a call from a stranger. The factories were in the middle of starting a new production line, so although he was in charge of the supply and demand of materials it was hard for him to get his head on straight. He'd been worried about how he should tell the construction site manager the news that the drive shaft that should've arrived ten days ago hadn't even shipped from the contractors.

"Are you Cho?"

Right off the bat, the caller on the line was hostile.

"Who's this?"

"Me, Chief Kim, from the site."

"And?"

"Why aren't you guys sending the goods?"

"The supplier is having a problem . . ."

He'd already heard that the new chief at the site had a bit of an attitude that "possibly required fixing."

"What kind of problem do you have that you're not even able to call to say things are delayed? And you still want us to finish by the deadline. Do you think we have some kind of magic wand that makes things happen?"

The on-site chief was implying that there must've been a deal going on with the supplier.

That was certainly a bolt from the blue, and he could feel the anger building up inside him. The caller couldn't care less and asked that the head of the department be put on the line, as if to say he was done talking to him. As if he'd committed a great wrong, the head of the department kept on repeating "sorry" like it was a song lyric. When he was done with the call, he called Cho into his office to grill him, which made him heated all over again. He figured he was the only one who could tame this mysterious beast who, as a mere on-site chief, dared to boss around a department manager at the headquarters. He made the call after discreetly crafting a plan, which was rare for him.

"Can you please put Kim on the line?"

He deliberately stressed "Kim" to emphasize that he was omitting the title, "Chief."

"That's me."

As he anticipated, Kim was quite unfriendly. Cho pressed his lips together. You don't use honorifics, I don't use honorifics.

"Well, it's me, deputy Cho, who you talked to earlier. Answer my question . . ."

It was deputy Cho instead of just Cho, and he said "answer my question" rather than "may I ask you a question." Korean disputes typically go through stages of arguing about the issue at hand, then to arguing about the honorifics, and in the end, arguing about each other's rude manners. As a result, the original issue never really matters in the end.

"Well? Hurry up. Don't pester me. I've got tons to do."

From Kim's brusque response, it seemed like he took the bait.

"You keep telling us to bring the shipment in quickly, but do you even have a place to unload the shipment? You're probably not even able to accept the shipment, so why do you have your panties in a bunch?"

"What the hell is this guy talking about?"

He took the bait! Cho's grip on the phone tightened.

"Who are you calling 'guy'? So, man, you think you can say anything you want because you're a chief?"

"What? Did you just say 'man'?"

"Yeah, being a chief doesn't make you my boss! Do you think all deputies are the same? Just how old are you?"

He felt somebody's finger poke him in his side, but he assumed it was a section chief in the office who was younger than he was.

"Yeah, get it through your head. In Korea, age still trumps any other issue in an argument. It makes you king, got it?" He calmly waited. After a moment of silence, the person on the other end of the line gave his final word.

"I'm college buddies with your director, your boss. Go ask him just how old I am."

Well, just how old is that? It was a question he simply couldn't ask his boss, who'd been looking down at him for a while now, his finger still pointing toward the sky.

THE MAN IN LOVE WITH TIME

THERE WAS A person who loved time more than life itself. This person couldn't bear to see time being wasted in an unnecessary way. He was a hardworking government employee who left his house at the exact same time every day, took the exact same amount of time to go to the train station, and took the train that left and arrived at the exact same times each day. When he arrived at his destination after the same amount of time had passed, he took the same amount of time to walk to his desk and sit down and work for the same amount of time. Every day, he left work at the same time as the day before, and arrived in front of the train station at the exact same time, purchased the exact same amount of liquor and snacks, and put them in the exact same plastic bag, walked the same way he always had, rode the exact same train, reviewed the day as he looked out the window for the exact same amount of time, drinking and snacking at the exact same pace, which put his mind at ease in the exact same way. He walked out the same aisle and exited the train through the exact same door, exchanged the same greetings that he'd repeat the next day with the train attendant, and he walked along the same path lined with flowers repeating the same song lyrics, "I wandered today to the hills, Maggie, to watch the scene below where we used to long, long ago," as he headed home.

As she had always done since the day they got married, his wife stood outside to welcome him home, and as always the couple told each other how their days went in soft voices, and they went into the house and sat down across from each other to have supper. Once supper was over, he had some time to himself before bedtime so he began to meditate about time.

He spent quite a lot of time thinking up the maxim, "Time is money," and was somewhat disappointed to find out an American named Benjamin Franklin had said it first. However, his feelings were restored as he smiled in satisfaction when he thought up "Time is the great physician." He'd have been happy for a while if Benjamin Disraeli had never existed. "Time is the longest distance between two places" was another he created, out of boredom, during his walk to the train station, but it so happened that the playwright Tennessee Williams had said something of the sort too. When he learned that, he made up "Time never stands still" (Tolstoy) there on the spot, and regardless of whether or not someone else said it first, he told his son about the saying, "Time is kind to those who use it well" (Schopenhauer). And on his wife's birthday, he gave her a card on which he wrote, "Time is like a fashionable host, that slightly shakes his parting guest by the hand, and with his arms outstretch'd, as he would fly, grasps in the comer; welcome ever smiles and farewell goes out sighing" (Shakespeare). On the cover of the card, it was printed, "Threefold the stride of time, from first to last! Loitering slow, the future creepeth, arrow-swift the present sweepeth, and motionless forever stands the past – Schiller." In the room where he meditated about time, Sima Qian's saying, "Time does not come twice. It comes to you every day but it is hard to gain and easy to lose," was hanging in a frame, without mention of the name Sima Qian. As you can see, he continuously conversed about time with scholars, writers, and historians, transcending the realm of time.

Then one day, he realized he was quite old. Everything surrounding him was also older than yesterday, than the first time he had it, than when he thought of this thought. His children grew and left home, finding jobs and settling down with their own families. His wife whom he loved and depended on unceasingly had wrinkles on her face and strands of white in her hair. She talked at a slower pace, felt pain in various places on her body, which she didn't know the cause of, and spent more time thinking about the past. From then on, he decided that he'd spend his life studying time. Let's borrow part of his knowledge to get a glimpse of time.

One of the longest units of time that humans have created is the kalpa. One kalpa is equal to one day in the time of the god Brahma. In human years, it's equal to four hundred and thirty-two million years. Sometimes it's used to express a long period of time which cannot be counted in human terms of years, months and days, and in this case, it refers to the cycle of time when heaven and earth open and on to its next reoccurrence. One kalpa also refers to the time it takes for an old man from the heavens to come down to earth and empty a mustard seed-filled circular fortress whose circumference is sixteen kilometers long, by taking one seed from it every three years. One small kalpa can refer to the amount of time it takes for a person who descends from the heavens once every three years to wear down a stone whose circumference is sixteen kilometers with his clothes which weigh three zhūs (zhū: unit of weight used during the Han dynasty of China, one zhū equals 1.55g). One medium kalpa is to carry out the same task, but with a stone of thirty-two kilometer's circumference. To do so with a stone of forty-eight kilometer's circumference is equal to one large kalpa. One small kalpa can also refer to the amount of time it takes for a person to start at the age of eighty-four thousand and lose one year of age every one hundred years to reach ten years in age, and then reverse the process to gain one year in age every one hundred years to become eighty-four thousand years old again. In these terms, twenty small kalpas is one medium kalpa, and four medium kalpas equal one large kalpa. Well, if we only live once, we ought to at least aspire to live this long.

Even a large kalpa, which is the universe's cycle to form, exist, be destroyed, and become extinct, and which is also the equivalent of twenty kalpas, is basically composed of the smallest unit of time called an instant (ksana= one thought= 1/75 sec). One hundred and twenty instants make up a tat-ksana (怛刹那), and sixty tat-ksanas make up one lava (臘縛) which is called muhūrta (牟呼栗多), and it is thirty muhūrtas that make up one day and one night (twenty-four hours). So, let's open our eyes and carefully search for any instant we could've neglected and dropped on the floor, so we can make it our own. One day, he spoke to me in a drunken tone on the train, holding a paper cup filled with soju.

"Sung, I've made an important discovery. People who live in high altitudes obtain more time than those who live at low altitudes."

According to the theory of relativity, if the time-lapse on the watch of a person living by the sea can be set as t, the time lapse of an observer on a mountain top moving at the speed of v can be expressed as t' = t(c=300,000km/sec), but due to the earth's rotation the person living by the sea ends up moving at a slower speed compared to the person living on a mountain top. According to the mathematical equation, it seems like an observer who moves at a faster speed will have more time than the observer with the slower speed. Let's all live on mountains. If we were to live a hundred years, we'd gain at least a few more minutes if we lived on the mountain than by the sea.

If your son is trying to decide on a job, recommend piloting so that he can spend more time at high altitudes. Actually, the occupation with the highest possibility of longevity is an astronaut. The closer their speed is to the speed of light, the slower their time seems to those who live on the earth's surface, satisfied with the mere speed of rotation of the earth. Our friends on space shuttles are not even close to the speed of light yet, but do move at a remarkably high speed. They are able to rotate along the earth if they maintain a speed of 7.9 kilometers per second (28,000 kilometers per hour), and if they reach 11.2 kilometers per second they can move beyond earth. At 16.7 kilometers per second they will be able to leave the solar system, and so far, manned space shuttles are in fact able to move beyond earth.

Furthermore, what would happen if a person could embark on a space shuttle that could move at a speed approaching the speed of light? The faster the speed, the slower his time would seem compared to a person left on earth. As a result, if it takes him a year to visit a supernova in the Cassiopia and come back home, civilization would disappear from the face of the earth. What a waste of time it'd seem like if he put in all this effort just to discover humans had become extinct and cockroaches had covered the face of the earth. He'd go crazy. He should've said good bye to the poplar tree back home when he had the chance!

"I see. I guess an excessively fast space shuttle would be harmful to one's health."

How much time does he have left? I was curious but didn't ask him. He not only despises any person, job, or world that makes him waste his time, he can't even spare the time to feel such disdain. He also doesn't like people who waste time asking useless questions. It's been quite a while since he studied time in his room by himself. Before he retired, he struggled with his government job to gain time. As a father he struggled with his son to gain time. As an old man he struggled with the futility of aging and sickness, and his compulsive obsessiveness regarding the fact that he didn't have much time left, in order to gain time. Now he devotes what time he has left to studying and saving time.

The day of a mayfly is as long as the lifespan of a mayfly. The year of an annual plant is as long and full of peril as the entire lifespan of an annual plant. I sincerely pray that every nanosecond (one-billionth of a second) he has is equal to one large kalpa!

THE TOILET

I'M TRYING TO recall which park it was. In downtown Seoul, there was a park frequented by many senior citizens. Next to it was an old Baduk club. There, the guests who came to play the board game were old, the owner was old and even the part-timers were old. The building itself was probably considerably old as well. I'm willing to bet that the owner of the building was an old person, too. The small, old, but steadfast building, holding its own among the surrounding wide and elongated buildings, reminded me of the obstinate old man who tries to hold on to himself even when the whole world is changing. Anyway, the fee for usage was only half of what they charged in other Baduk clubs. Next to the Baduk club was an ageing but clean restroom that seemed to get meticulous attention from an industrious old man. When I entered it, I saw a piece of paper with a message written on it, on the wall above the men's urinal. It was graceful, written with care, but the slight trembling in the letters showed that it was probably written by the shaky hand of a senior.

"Just one step forward."

"Please flush after you pee-pee."

FURLOUGH

THERE WERE TWO countries looking across the border at one another. The two countries didn't want to acknowledge that the other was a country. That was because they were originally one and the same. They were always at each other's throats. Unable to take it anymore, the people of the respective countries drew an invisible line between them and built a red brick house right on it. In this house was a long table and the invisible line ran down the middle of the table. At times, the representatives of each country held meetings, sitting on either side of the table, careful not to step over the line.

"Don't cross the line."

"If you cross the line, we'll kill you."

"Don't worry about us. Worry about yourselves."

That was the unchanging subject of the meeting for decades. Inside that house, not even an ant was able to step over the line. As soon as the children of the two countries learned about the invisible line, they'd mimic it and make lines of their own. Don't come to my school. Don't come to my house. Don't trespass into my area. They'd even dig a deep line with a utility knife into desks used by two people and ruthlessly attack whatever crossed the line. The children who learned and practiced this behavior would eventually become soldiers and representatives protecting the invisible line.

Behind each side of the house that was built on top of the invisible line were the two flapping flags of each country. The flags would be raised at sunrise and lowered at sunset. Whenever this happened, the generals and soldiers of the two countries would solemnly salute their respective flags. Sometimes, the generals would briefly lock eyes but they never exchanged any greetings. They'd immediately turn around to their own side. Time passed uneventfully. Things remained the same for dozens of years.

People, I guess, are maybe able to dodge and to bear the arrow of time since the body has elasticity, and it can move and hide. Flagpoles, on the other hand, are hard. They don't have feet to move, and they can't think of hiding, so they're unable to bear the infinity of time. One day, the base of the ball-shaped finial which was sitting on top of the flagpole of the Eastern country began to succumb to the harsh treatment of time and wind. A soldier of the Eastern country climbed up the flagpole. Maybe he was hung up on something else or he was distracted, but the new finial ended up being placed higher than before. As a result, the flagpole of the Eastern country was a little taller than the Western country's flagpole. The next morning, the blue flag of the Eastern country hung higher than the white flag of the Western country.

The next day, the general of the Western country was saluting his country's flag when he noticed that the Eastern country's flag was just the tiniest bit higher than it was the day before. This man was known to have a very sharp eye and was the type who didn't like to lose. The general immediately called in his chief of staff and ordered him to come up with a plan. The man thought about it and sent up an idle soldier to the top of their own flagpole. The soldier broke the perfectly fine finial and slid back down, pretending that it'd been an accident. Another soldier swiftly climbed up and installed a new finial with a slightly longer neck. For some reason, he got the idea to install the finial higher than the Eastern country's finial, rather than place it at an equal height. As a result, the flag of the Western country was now just a bit higher than the Eastern country's flag.

A few days passed, and the general of the Eastern country was spitting toward the Western country's flag, when he suddenly noticed that the height of the other country's flag had changed. This general was known for not being very shrewd, and being as stubborn as a bull. He kicked his chief of staff in the shins and yelled orders to come up with a plan. The chief of staff chose the skinniest soldier from a group of soldiers who were standing around in a sunny spot, smoking, and ordered him to ascend the flagpole. The soldier spat into his palms and climbed up the swaying flagpole. He took off the finial and inserted a long iron stick before re-installing the finial on top of it. That soldier nearly earned a furlough as a reward. That is, if a leaner and quicker soldier from the Western country hadn't climbed up his side's flagpole less than a day later. However, right before that soldier was about to receive an honorary title, he had to witness a leaner soldier with longer limbs from the Eastern country make it up his side's flagpole and hang his country's flag higher than the Western country's.

From that day on, soldiers from the two countries climbed up and down their flagpoles every day. The flagpoles grew taller and taller and began to sway from side to side, looking like they would break any minute. Soldiers would slip down and injure themselves from climbing.

"Sir, we must use a ladder."

"Not before the other side does!"

"We must at least initiate a human pyramid strategy."

"I said, not before the other side does!"

At the end of a long day, the generals reported to their respective headquarters. The conclusions of the reports were identical, as if they'd been written together. "This is an invisible war. Requesting backup. Calling for emergency backup."

Emergency meetings were held in the two countries' commanding headquarters. Generals would select the best and most fearless tree climbers among their soldiers and send them on trucks to the house that was built on top of the invisible line. The area surrounding the brick house was crawling with skinny soldiers who resembled monkeys. The soldiers were ordered to starve in order to decrease their body weight. Hunger was to be overcome with a sense of duty, patriotism, and the faith that "anything is possible." The flagpoles kept on growing taller.

Eventually a soldier from the Eastern country who looked like a spider fell to the ground and died while working on adding height to the flagpole. He did however complete his mission before his death. The Eastern flagpole soared as high as humanly possible.

A heated discussion ensued in the military headquarters of the Western country. One general presented the idea of crossing over into the Eastern territory at night to blow up the flagpole. Then there was also the idea of digging an underground cave to the pole and knocking it over. All these ideas were only possible if they crossed the invisible line, but not only was that against the treaty, it was also a disgrace. One general said they should bring in a monkey. One general said that his brother worked at a zoo and he swore that you couldn't find a monkey that was trained to fix a flagpole in any zoo in the whole world. One general received disapproving glares when he said that they should remove their own flagpole, since they were fighting a losing battle. It was plain to see that he'd be disadvantaged at his next promotion. Each second passed in agony and despair. The general of the engineering battalion slapped his hand down on the table as he suggested that they use a crane. An admiral of the navy said they should incorporate helicopters. One general who was a former fireman mumbled that an aerial ladder would be better. The Army Chief of Staff shook his head, saying that if it became known that they were mobilizing heavy equipment just to heighten a flagpole, they'd be the laughingstock of not only their enemy state but also the world. Generals, chiefs of staff, soldiers, secretaries, presidents, and all patriots who became aware of the secret of the invisible war, all in their own way, squeezed out as many ideas as they could.

That's how the Private first class who wreaked havoc by placing the finial higher than it should've been, was granted a furlough. His idea was illustrated as such:

1) Cut the bottom part of the flagpole with a saw
2) Lay down the flagpole
3) Extend the pole as needed
4) Install the finial
5) Erect the flagpole and connect it to the severed part
6) Hang the flag

Everybody's mouth was agape. And then they shouted, "Yeah!"

Along with a medal, he was granted a furlough as a reward. He was away from summer to winter before he returned to his base. When he returned, the flagpoles on either side had shrunk to the appropriate height. They say nobody so much as glanced toward the flagpoles.

SURVEILLANCE

DURING A VISIT to a restroom, I once was directly faced with a wall covered with colorful graffiti. The scribblings included everything from simple philosophical musings to jokes, but the majority consisted of descriptions of sexual experiences, curses condemning the immorality of the scribbling, objections to those curses, and criticism regarding those objections. Among them, right smack in the middle of the wall, in big, handsomely written letters that prevailed over them all, was the manager's scribbling.

Warning
No Graffiti
Surveillance Camera in Operation!
Posted by Manager

BIG APPETITE

1

A RECORDING OF what can be called a glutton sighting, which I witnessed myself, involved some high school students who lived away from home. Luckily I was in time to watch them prepare a meal when I visited their room. One person was busy opening packets of ramen noodles and sequentially separating the seasoning and the noodles that were inside the packet. Another person chopped green onions and cracked and whisked the eggs. The iron pot they were using was taken out of an electronic rice cooker designed to cook for seven people. On all sides of the rooms, ramen boxes were stacked to the ceiling, half of them full and half of them empty. Thanks to the ramen boxes, there wasn't much space for a desk or a dresser, and all of their textbooks, daily items, and clothes were placed inside the ramen boxes. The ramen box was their table, their cooking counter, and their trash can where they threw away what was left after washing the dishes. Since they inhaled every last drop of the broth, dishwashing would simply consist of removing any leftover oil in the pot. The oil could simply be wiped with toilet paper, which could be thrown away in a ramen box. And that was only when there was time in between meals, for the meals would rapidly commence, one after another.

When I asked them if they needed anything, one of them replied, "I think we could use a large bowl. We have only one pot, so if one person's hogging it, the next person has no choice but to wait. We sometimes fight over who goes first. It's a drag and I really don't like that."

"Are you saying that one person will eat nine packets of ramen?"

"Yeah. Mom said we can't get a larger pot. I wanted to buy another one, but she said we wouldn't be able to afford tuition because of the ramen costs."

They told me that the largest number of ramens one of them had eaten was seventeen. It was during the festival period at a nearby college. A group of college students left when their soccer team had lost, leaving behind all of the pre-ordered ramen, so this individual ended up finishing all of it by himself. Not the broth, of course.

2

I DIDN'T MEET, was only told of, this other glutton who's also a high school student. Unlike the students in the previous story, this student had an apparent reason for having a big appetite. He was an up-and-coming Korean-style wrestler in a high school known for the sport, the sport of Ssireum. His bodyweight was more than double that of an average high school student, so it was only natural that he ate twice as much.

The father of this Ssireum player was a simple government employee in a rural area, and his only dream in life was to see his son become a Cheonhajangsa—the strongest man under the sky, a title given to the strongest Ssireum player in the country—and bring home a golden calf, the grand prize for the title. However, he couldn't handle his son's food bill with his pittance of a salary, so this wish was likely to remain just that, a wish. Thanks to his unrealizable dream, his hair grew silver before his colleagues' hair, and he always looked depressed and formed a habit of sighing. When his colleagues at work learned of his situation, they all agreed to support this young Ssireum player. Their plan was to take turns each month taking the Ssireum player out for dinner. And the first person to do so was the person who told me this story.

The place he met up with the father and son was the largest bulgogi restaurant in the small town. Conscious of his son, the father, who was as skinny as a stick, carefully suggested, in a barely audible voice, that they go to a cheaper nearby restaurant selling pork short ribs. His colleague raved that he was there to help out his troubled friend, that he was more than ready for any size bill, and so he ordered ten servings of bulgogi. The father couldn't focus on eating, instead just repeated the motion of picking up and putting down his chopsticks. The colleague barely ate one serving, aghast at the amount the young athlete was gobbling down. In other words, the young Ssireum player ate the majority of the bulgogi. He didn't once glance away from the food, nor take his mouth away, nor lift his head. As time passed, the father became more fidgety. The colleague put him at ease and ordered ten more servings.

"How's that? Do you think this'll be enough?" he asked the Ssireum player when he finished the second round of bulgogi. After finishing all the meat, the young wrestler was looking down at the table, rubbing away at some drops of water there with the tip of his finger. Though it wasn't hot at all in the restaurant, beads of sweat kept rolling down his father's face. His colleague figured that he wasn't satisfied yet, so he suggested they go to another place. They stepped outside and the father approached him as he looked around for a pork barbecue restaurant.

"This wouldn't have happened if we'd just started at a cheaper pork barbecue restaurant. I'm so sorry . . ."

"Please, we're just getting started. I'm taking care of tonight's meal. Come to think of it, pork isn't any less nutritious, and the tender cuts can be quite delicious."

He entered a pork barbecue joint, guided by the father and son. The young wrestler continued to be silent and the father seemed less worried. The colleague confidently told them to order as much as they wanted. In truth, he was slowly becoming worried about his thinning wallet. The young wrestler mumbled something as he furtively glanced at his father.

"What did he say?"

"He says he can't eat much because he feels guilty. He asked me to order for him."

"Well, do it."

"Should I? I'm so sorry about all of this . . ."

The father asked the waitress to bring fifteen servings of pork barbecue all at once. He didn't want to inconvenience her with multiple trips. This time, he didn't pick up his chopsticks either. All he did was take sips of the kimchi broth. The young wrestler moved with lightning speed, as he laid three to four pieces of lettuce on his palm, which was as big as an iron pot lid, and placed more than ten pieces of pork on top, proceeding then to stuff it all into his mouth. As he chewed and swallowed, he'd already be layering more lettuce on his palm. It was only when this frightful meal was over that the young wrestler seemed satisfied at last. At that moment, the waitress approached them. She asked them their choice for the side dish that came with the pork, either rice or buckwheat noodles in cold broth. The colleague ordered the noodles. The young wrestler whispered something to his father once again.

"What did he say?"

The father had trouble opening his mouth to relay what his son had said.

"He asked if we couldn't have rice . . ."

"Oh, yes, let's have rice. Have a lot. Eating is the only thing that'll make you grow bigger and taller. Well then, what do you want?"

The young wrestler shyly looked up at his father's colleague.

"May I have bibimbap?"

"Of course. Excuse me, bring us an especially hearty serving of bibimbap."

The father looked up at the ceiling, letting out long sighs. The young wrestler looked at his father for a while and when he decided his father wasn't going to help him, he spoke up about what he wanted.

"Um, could you make that two bibimbaps?"

Two bowls of bibimbap were served while the colleague's jaw dropped open. The young wrestler lifted one bowl and dumped it into another, as if he were throwing down his opponent in a Ssireum match. Next, he mixed two servings worth of bibimbap and finished it in the blink of an eye. The colleague forgot about the bowl of buckwheat noodles set in front of him, and sat dumbfounded watching the young wrestler finish the rice. The young wrestler wiped the beads of sweat off his nose and asked, "Dad, do we have dinner plans for tomorrow, too?"

3

THIS TIME, IT'S my fantasy of a glutton. The story's actually about a family, not an individual. This one's also about a father and son, but what's different about them is that both have big appetites. I heard his wife talk about it.

"My side of the family is skinny as toothpicks. My parents are small eaters. And like my parents, my siblings all habitually nibble at their food. When I met my husband, it was so refreshing to see him devour everything with enthusiasm. I did think he ate a bit much on our honeymoon. And then I found out he had a giant appetite, but it was too late. Most of our income goes to food. It's not like we eat gourmet food. Most of our side dishes consist of kimchi, and because even that gets to be too much sometimes, we usually have rice with sides of rice . . . My family owns a rice farm, so when we first got married, we used to receive rice from them. We had eight in our family, which became seven when I got married and moved out. What my family consumes in a month, the two of us consume in ten days. I couldn't continue to receive rice from my family because I felt like they thought I was taking too much. Since then, my husband's salary has all gone toward buying rice. We walk most distances, and most of our clothes are so stitched up that there isn't anywhere left to stitch. The first time I ever got in a taxi after I got married was when I went to the hospital to give birth to our child. Once that child grew big enough, he started eating at an incredible pace. I guess the size of one's appetite is also hereditary. The first rice bowl my son had, after weaning off breast milk at three, was as big as an adult's. When he turned seven, he ate half as much as his father. I had no choice but to find a job. Who watches the kid, you ask? All he needs is rice. As long as I leave a pot of cooked rice with him, he can play by himself. I worked as a housemaid but that didn't cut it, so I found a job at a restaurant. I figured the leftover rice or side dishes that I could bring home might help. That lasted for about a minute. These days, the restaurant owner gives me funny looks. I mean, the leftover food is going to dogs or pigs. And I don't want my family to seem like dogs or pigs, so I can't bring home a lot of rice. The way we live is below human standards. I can't figure out how food ruined our lives. I don't know what's going to happen to us . . . Is my husband a big man? No. Just slightly larger than average. My son is a little bigger than other kids. I'm, as you can see, thin. Me? Well, I do eat more than what I used to when I was a newlywed. Yes. About five bowls of rice per meal. What happened to me, you ask? I don't know. I just don't know . . ."

THE WISH

I'M NOT VERY familiar with golf, but I do know how it can drive a person crazy. I actually know a person who's caught up in it, almost to the point of craziness. He's already past the age of seventy. His son is the school friend of my friend's brother-in-law. I met this son of his in my friend's brother-in-law's office. The office, located inside a shabby six-story building in one of the alleys around Namdaemun, was as worn as could be, without one single piece of intact furniture. When my friend introduced me, his brother-in-law yawned as if his mouth were gaping open like that of the old dog I saw sauntering around the building, and handed me his business card. The card indicated that the office was the headquarters of the Mainland Trading slash Mainland Development slash Mainland Consulting companies, that the address was Namdaemun Road, which was the most central of all the central regions in Korea, and that the owner of the business card was the CEO and president, etc. I wondered if the office could be sufficient for a trading, development, and consulting firm. If he was the CEO, that meant he represented board members, so although there should've been other board members, there wasn't even an errand girl in sight. Well, these details aren't what's important.

"Why do they just leave such a rundown building in the middle of such an expensive neighborhood? If they built a higher building and leased the offices, the rent would be at least ten times what it is now."

He must've been bored, because when my friend said that, he started explaining.

The owner of the building was an old man who was over seventy years old. He not only owned that building, but also several others in the principal downtown area, and also an extraordinarily large piece of land planned for development in the surrounding area of Seoul. His wife was well over sixty years old and had started to attend church in recent years. The last time she went to church, she gave a tithe, which was about one ten-thousandth of his annual income. And the next day, she checked into a hospital. Why?

The CEO said she'd been beaten by her husband. It all started when the husband yelled at her, asking how she dared give an offering without asking him first, and the wife talked back. She allegedly mumbled that she'd lived her whole life serving an impossible miser and tyrant of a husband who demanded that she seek permission to buy even a bag of beansprouts or a lump of tofu, so what was the big deal about spending a lousy twenty to thirty thousand won without permission? Her only wish was to have just one million won to spend as she wished. That's when the husband came running out of the room with a golf club in his hand, and beat his wife to the point of having to check her into the hospital. In the end, it unfortunately turned out that the hospital bills amounted to a lot more than what his wife tithed to the church, and what he said was, "I am okay with spending money doing what I wish to do, but I can't bear to see money going into something I don't want to do."

His son oversaw the downtown building, one of the old man's many real estate assets, but all that overseeing entailed was to collect monthly rent. That's how much I'd heard when this son entered the office. In a spiffy black suit with brief case in hand, he plopped down into a chair without even saying hello.

"It's so hot that I don't think I can do this shit anymore. Where's the air conditioner?"

"The one we installed when we opened the office? We took it down the next day so that the vibration wouldn't bring the entire building down, remember?"

"I don't know if it's because the economy's in a slump, but nobody pays their rent on time these days. I just might get my joints knocked out by my father again."

Judging from the way he so candidly talked in front of a stranger about what could be considered an embarrassing experience, perhaps he was the kind of man that lacked prudence and caused trouble that earned him beatings by a golf club from his father. He took my business card and continued to talk while fanning himself with it.

"The people I envy the most are people who have business cards. I would die to have a business card."

"You mean you collect hundreds of million won a month but you don't even have a business card?"

"I did print out some business cards recently. My friend here talked me into doing it. Thanks to that I almost had my forehead knocked in by my dad's golf club."

The story went like this. Because the building was so old and costing too much in maintenance fees and low rents, there was someone who wanted to rebuild it. The down payments that'd come from building and renting out a new building would alone pay for the construction, and the monthly rents would be several times the amount of the down payments. It'd be the same conclusion by anyone's calculation. However, the reason why the old man's son accepted this suggestion was that he'd be able to print a business card with the words "Development" or "Trading" on it. That was his one wish. Anyway, he got caught two days after he had the business cards printed. The old man immediately took out the problematic golf club and shook it in front of his son's eyes, shouting.

"You bum, who told you that you were good enough to open a business? If you keep this up, you can be sure you won't be seeing a penny from me, even if I drop dead tomorrow. You're a good for nothing with nothing but empty ideas in your head . . . If it crumbles, it's still my building to see crumble. If you so much as lay a finger on the building, I'll donate it to the government. You got that?"

After telling that story, he sighed and asked his friend, that is, my friend's brother-in-law, "Hey, do you still have any of those business cards left?"

My friend's brother-in-law rustled around in his desk drawer and handed him the one business card he said he'd saved as a souvenir. It was handed to me and I saw it had the company names, Mainland Trading, Mainland Development, and Mainland Consulting, the address on Namdaemun Road, and the name of the board director on it. In essence, he rented the office out to his friend for free so that he could have a business card for himself. Of course, his father would go crazy if he found out.

I know nothing about golf. However, I do know someone who's consumed by it. I bumped into an old man on the bus one day. I was on my way to go fishing, so I had my fishing bag with me. The old man also had something that looked like a fishing bag, so I talked to him. However, what he had inside his bag were golf clubs. I intuitively knew that this old man was the father of my friend's brother-in-law's friend. He is, as far as I know, the only person in Korea who'd go to a golf club by taking an intercity bus.

"How can I reach a single-digit handicap? I'd die a happy man right now if I could figure out how to do it."

That's what he said when we were about to go our separate ways with our respective bags.

THE CRABS OF ARCADIA

THE ISLAND OF Arcadia, which is a territory of Belgium, is famous for its freshwater crab. This crab, which is called the crab of Arcadia, originated about forty million years ago and has continued to prosper on the island, but according to the natives, there isn't any other species that's deemed as useless as this crab. The crab's small size makes it a hassle to catch, and even if you did catch one, it'll either plaster a smelly foam on the sides of the boat, damaging the mesh of the net, or scratch or tear the soles of the fishermen's feet. If you were to roast one, all you'd get is bitter-tasting flesh the size of a fingernail, so nobody bothers to catch them. There's no fish that likes this kind of crab nor does it have any natural enemies. Some speculate that this may be the reason they've survived for so long.

By nature, the crab of Arcadia eats only a small amount, defecates a small amount, and moves as little as possible. It has one mating season in its entire lifespan, but quietly completes fertilization without any change in color or demeanor. When the female and male can't find each other due to deterioration of the environment, asexual reproduction has also been observed. Once fertilization is over, the female lays its eggs in a hole dug by clams or fish, and goes without eating until the eggs hatch. No fish or clam tries to enter the hole when the crab is in it. That's because they fear the crab's pincers, which are stronger than a blade and sharper than a spear. As such, the crab has the perfect traits for survival and propagation, but there seems to be a reason why it can't become the dominant species of the island of Arcadia.

A wise man who was born and lived until his death on the east side of the island once recorded on a sea shell, "It exists and lives alone, is useless, and so is able to live for long periods of time untouched by calculations of gain and loss and hardship." But according to a historian living on the west side of the island, the wise man was just beautifying and likening his own needlessly long life to the crab's, and what he said had nothing to do with the crab. He also criticized the wise man for only seeing the life of the crab and not its death.

Thanks to the sturdy shell of the crab, which is harder than any protection nature has given to another life form on Arcadia, the crab doesn't need to fear any attack. Also, the pincers, which are made of the same substance, allow the crab to mercilessly dig into and cut any type of shell. So, the historian records the following.

"The crab of Arcadia only dies at the claw of another crab of Arcadia. The moment they meet, they smash their shell and claws against one another and exchange deadly wounds. Such brutal blades are hidden in the grace provided by nature."

THE AMUSING LIFE - 3
On Violence

I AM A lucky person. I've never been hit by anyone. I am a lucky person to have lived a life without once being hit in this land where violence is found everywhere. Actually, I've been hit once. That's why I'm a lucky person. I've been hit only once. In a land where violence prevails, such as violence in schools, violence outside of schools, clubs promoting violence, gangs, violent language, violence-wielding groups, anti-violence, non-resistance, etc., I am a lucky person to only have been hit once in my life.

The story begins when I was in junior high school. I moved and transferred schools from the countryside to Seoul, the outskirts of Seoul, to the land of fists where there lived a sickening number of people and where twice as many fists were always ready to offer a punch. The land where I lived before I transferred, my hometown where I'd attended elementary school, was a land where lambs and lions played together. In that land, if you showed a shred of violence, you were beaten to death on the spot. There was no concept of using violence to survive and make a living. If it was difficult to make a living, you didn't live. It wasn't my choice to move away from that land. It probably wasn't the will of God. I can't believe that he'd transfer me to the land of fists just to lead me into temptation.

Anyway, just a few days after I started middle school in the land of fists, I was asked to go on an errand. The kid who sent me on the errand was three or four years older than myself, yet he was in the same grade, and was a bully well-known among the area's elementary schools, middle schools, high schools, institutes where kids who'd failed their university entrance exam studied, and even vocational schools. I don't understand why a bully of such greatness would send me, a naïve, pale boy who'd just transferred from the countryside, to "go fetch some bread and soda from the store." I guess only God knew. Any other kid would've thought, "Ah, the opportunity has come. He gave me the honor of fetching him something, so I shall bring back some snacks with all of my life" and run with clenched fists. But I had no intention of doing that. Why? I was a babe in the woods. I was from the country of lambs and lions. I was an idiot. So I refused the errand.

"I don't want to."

I can never forget the look on that kid's face. It was a somewhat embarrassed, somewhat dumbfounded, somewhat annoyed, somewhat bewildered look, and I'd later recognize that look again on the face of the barracks leader in my military days who'd communicate with his club, and of the president who announced a tough crackdown in the days when demonstrations swept through the cities. It was the look that emerges right before someone asks, "Are you a soldier? Are you a student? Who the hell are you? Are you even human?" The look that appears right before violence begins.

Of course, I was beaten. I was dragged outside behind the restroom wall and beaten for a good hour, teased by kids who were smaller than me, weaker than me, who came here before I did. Do you know kids who never apologize even when they are beaten to death? There are adults who'd rather die standing than live on their knees. That was the way I took the full beating, standing up, with no end in sight. After that happened, I decided I'd never be beaten again and stuck to my plan. I am a lucky person. Putting this plan into action, I was able to survive. In this very kingdom of violence.

How'd I do it? For example, what do you do when you're a freshman and the seniors in the weightlifting club of your high school lock the front and back of your classroom to give the entire class a taste of the bat? For example, what do you do when your scary-looking Korean teacher gives your class an hour to memorize the *Gwandong Byeolgok*, a poem written in Old Korean by Songgang Jung Chul, and comes back in exactly an hour to hit the students who don't have it memorized? What do you do when you're walking along a deserted path behind the school, and bump into gang members from the neighboring high school where many delinquent students attended, who push a fork in front of your face and ask you for bus tokens or money to buy ramen? You scramble, is what you do. You open the window and jump. If the window doesn't open, you break it and run. If your bag is too heavy, leave it and run. So what if you break your leg? So what if the window breaks? So what if you get billed for the hospital, for the window, for a new bag? It's better than being a victim of violence. It costs you much less. A person who wields violence can forget about it easily, but the person on the receiving end of it will shudder throughout his life because of the terror of the moment. Above all, it's bad because violence breeds more violence. The solution is to scramble. It's beneficial for both parties.

When I first transferred to my middle school in the land of fists, I was a slowpoke who ran a hundred meters in twenty seconds. When I ran after the first time I was beaten, my record was shortened by two seconds. By the time I graduated it was shortened by another two seconds. When I was a freshman in high school, I could brag about my fast feet, which ran a hundred meters in thirteen seconds, and within the year, I was in the eleven-second club. A soccer player who was considered as good as any member of the national team was the only person who had quicker feet than me, but by the time I'd graduated, I was faster than he was, too. That soccer player found out that there was an ordinary student who was faster than him, and came after me with his fist, which helped nudge me into the ten-second arena.

Finally, I became a member of the national team for track and field, and was given the honor of representing my country, wearing my flag in a neck-to-neck race with scramblers from all the other countries. If ever you find yourself on the verge of being victimized by violence at school, outside of school, near a learning center, inside or outside your home, please remember me. The guy who scrambles away at the sound of fanfare and the cheers of the crowd. You can do it, too.

THE BRICK

AS YOU KNOW, I served my military duty in Seoul. Let's just say it was a small, special-forces team. Land is expensive in Seoul, so the military bases are small and don't allow for much space for various facilities. In other words, there were no saunas on site, and so we were given a small bath allowance in our monthly wages. On Sundays, we were allowed bath outings. Since it was the military, the higher ranked officers would be the ones to go. Of course, the lower ranked officers wanted a sniff of the sweet air of the outside world more badly. The pitiful lower ranks were allowed to leave base only for church. There they could pray to God to let them climb the ranks faster. I was a low ranking officer at first, too. I was almost going crazy wanting to get out of the base. But still I didn't go to church. I wasn't a Christian, and I thought it'd be low to lie about that.

There was a high ranking officer who I became friends with pretty quickly. He was a big guy and ate like a horse. He ate three or four times the amount an ordinary person did. I was able to become friends with him because I worked in the kitchen. He wasn't a man of many words. When he spoke, the words he said meant something. He never said anything useless. This guy never missed a trip to the bathhouse when he became one of the high-ranks. I guess he had a lot of dirt to get off since he was big, so he had to wash more often.

But listen. Whenever he returned from a bath, his whole body would be red. Not only his face, but even down to his toenails, crimson red. I think it was about a fifteen-minute walk from the bathhouse to the base? You'd think his body would pretty much cool down walking that distance. Another guy told me that he'd only stay in the steam room when he visited the bathhouse. All the others didn't have the stamina for it, running on military food. People in the military usually didn't want to lose the fat that sustained them because training is so rough. Also, he'd never miss his visit even in the summer. He said showers just didn't do it for him. He'd go use the sauna for a steam-out, even in the summer. So you can imagine how hungry he'd get. He'd eat like crazy when he returned. So much so that people would gawk at him. I always saved enough leftovers for him. I guess he was thankful for that. He told me something before he was discharged from his duty.

"Private Ryu. I want to thank you for what you've done for me. I don't have anything to give you but I'll let you in on a tip that'll help you pass time during your service. You know that bathhouse? If you go there, go into the sauna. Don't sit on the chair, but rather on the floor and think about why I was always in that sauna in the summers and winters."

That was all. I told you he was a man of few words. And then he left the military. When he left, it was my turn to take Sunday trips to the bathhouse. The first day that I made my trip was in early summer. I went to the bathhouse nearest to the base, but it was so shabby. The chimney was the only thing that was presentable in the building, tall as any factory chimney. It looked like it'd been more than thirty years since it was built. It was not only small, but old, too. It was summer, so we were the only customers there. Anyway, a small group of us, five or six high ranking officers, entered the bathhouse single-file. I took a quick shower and went into the sauna room. It was dingy. Yet as dingy as it was, it was steamy and hot as hell. The other guys that'd come with me didn't care to enter it twice. I sat down on the floor of the sauna like my former superior officer told me to. And I remembered what he said. Think of him? What the heck could be here? You couldn't have given me any details? And I lay on my back, but hold on, look here. In the shadow underneath the long bench attached to the wall, there was a brick that caught my eye. The others were stacked sideways, but this one was not and stuck out. I reached in and grabbed it and tried to move it. What do you know, it moved. I pulled it out, and huh, it came out. What else is there to do but peer through the hole? It turned out it connected to the women's sauna.

I'm telling you, slender legs were walking this way and that, although I really couldn't see that well because of the steam. Of course, I could only see up to the knees. The brick was very low down on the wall. If I wanted to see more I had to push my face against the hole, and I was going nuts. My face was nearly getting squashed. Those bricks weren't just hot, they were sizzling hot. I almost got burned trying to get a fuller peek. Breathing wasn't easy, either. I put the brick back in its place and ran out of there. I dove into the cold water tub like a seal. I left it at that on that day.

Afterward, I never missed a trip to the bathhouse. Come winter, summer, snow or rain. The most amazing thing I saw through that hole in the wall was . . . One day, I was startled to find that the brick had already been taken out. I immediately thought someone else had discovered this secret. But that wasn't it. The brick wasn't on my side. Someone on the other side had taken out the brick. That's right . . . It was someone from the women's bath. I guess she'd pulled it out since it was protruding. How dumbfounded we were when the two of us, through the hole, directly locked eyes. For some reason, I felt something like sadness. Not sadness itself, just something like sadness.

Before my military duty ended, I pulled aside the low ranking soldier who used to save a lot of leftovers for me for whenever I returned from the bathhouse.

"Private Sung. Thank you for all you've done. I don't have anything to give you but I'll give you a tip to stay unbored while you complete your military service. You know the bathhouse near here? When you go there, go into the sauna. Don't sit on the bench but on the floor and think about why I always went to the sauna in the summer and the winter."

Recently, I happened to pass by the bathhouse. It was now a commercial building with a supermarket on the basement level. It still had that chimney, though. You know, the kind of brick chimney that stands high with the sauna symbol on it, with the word "Bath" written on it. The chimney was still there, standing like a watchtower on a brick fortress. Why would they have saved that one thing? I'm suddenly curious why.

THE DRAGON OF THE STREAM

IT WAS THE first time I'd seen him since graduation, so it must've been something like fifteen years ago that I saw him last. We met inside a tent bar on the street in a neighborhood well-known for being inhabited by people studying for national qualification exams, thanks to its plethora of specialized test prep centers and such. He was still studying for a national qualification exam, and still had the habit of stopping by a tent bar in the late night hours for a bowl of noodles, whenever he had had a drink. (This was also a habit I shared.) So naturally, in that neighborhood, at that time of night, that'd be the only place where we'd meet. He was sitting alone, eating his noodles, gazing at the Sae stream, the stream that wrapped around the so-called "state exam village," overpopulated with pythons dreaming of fulfilling their sky-high ambitions.

Where could I've gotten the silly idea that at nearly forty he'd still be challenging himself to pass the national exam? He was the typical diligent student. Whenever test time rolled around, not only would he memorize every question that'd been on the test in the past few decades, but he'd also obtain practice tests to strategize even more perfectly. However, if there was a question on the test that dealt with material that he wasn't able to memorize or practice, he couldn't write a single word. He hadn't been able to improve on his inflexibility or compulsive personality, so it was no wonder he hadn't passed the test even at the age of forty. When he got his first report card in college twenty years ago, he said, "That's strange. You spend far more time at cafes and bars than I do studying at the library, but how do we end up with the same grades?"

Even that seemed to be a subject of study to him. I gave him a piece of advice.

"Listen, my friend. In this world, there are things you can achieve by studying, and things you can't. School exams are also a part of this world, so just studying textbooks won't cut it. Well, you're the type of person to start dating only after you've fully studied how to date and love. I'll give you an opportunity to preview the material. Let's go dancing."

"Do me a favor. You go out and enjoy life for the both of us."

That was his answer. It'd been fifteen years since we met, but I felt a little bad because I didn't feel like I danced and enjoyed life enough for the both of us.

"You know, my eyesight has suffered trying to look for your name on the list of the final applicants for the national exam. Didn't they increase the quota recently? I'm going to need glasses or something."

He let out a bitter laugh as he accepted the drink I handed him.

"You're right. This is like prison. It's a one-half square meter cell that I locked myself into all because of this ambition to maneuver into high society in one sweep. And I've been serving time for twenty years. Ah, that's one-third of my life dedicated to this futility."

"If you know that, why are you still here?"

"Guys like us, our dream is all about going from nothing to becoming the great dragon, even if it costs us all this trouble.

It's not like we can give up on that now. Besides, what'll other people think?"

"What good is a trembling grandfather of a dragon with a walking cane, after being locked up twenty years in prison? If you spent that kind of time and dedication running a tent bar, you would've become a millionaire by now."

Right then, I saw the owner of the tent bar turn his head toward us. My friend said, "Some people stay an owner of a tent bar no matter how long they work at it, be it twenty or fifty years."

The owner of the tent bar blinked his wide eyes like a fish laying on a cutting board about to be sliced up for sashimi, and interjected as if he couldn't take it anymore, "No adding the bill to your tab today. Absolutely not."

SOLITUDE

AT TIMES I feel like the men's sauna is a place you pay to go
to feel daunted. You see burly guys with protruding biceps and
six-pack abs strutting around, arms bent like bows. And then
there are the handsome ones with bodies that are even more
flawless than their faces. Guys who smile at themselves in the
mirror as they lather shampoo into their hair like movie stars.
Also, looking at the guys who run out of the sauna and dive into
the cold tub to swim like seals intimidates guys like me who
quiver in hot water and shiver in cold water. And on days that
there are running, jumping, and shouting kids, I hide myself
away and sit in a far corner so that I won't fall over or get water
splashed on me. On just such a day, I was washing myself in a
corner of the bath house. When I took a look around, I spotted
a large man on the opposite side of the hot bath, washing himself in solitude. Nobody attempted to go near him. It was as if
there were an invisible boundary that enclosed the biceped guys,
handsome men, and playful kids all on my side. Whenever the
kids ended up near the man while running around, they'd stop
in their tracks and walk quietly by, looking terrified. Unable
to endure the annoyance of the biceps, handsomes, and kids
any longer, I found myself inching toward the area where the
man was. I was envious of and fascinated by this man who sat

proud and dignified, not caring about anyone else, as he bathed
in this wide, peaceful area all by himself. The man looked into
empty space as he scrubbed himself with a washing mitt. His
hard-pressed lips, dark eyebrows, hardened stare, stubby short
hair, and big and small scars all over his body kind of gave you
some clues about his personality or questionable occupation. At
any rate, thanks to him, I was able to have a more relaxed bath.
The man didn't pay the least attention to whether I was there or
not. He must've finished scrubbing because he stood up with a
grunt. I realized he was much larger than I thought. And that's
when my eyes fell on an intimidating tattoo that was on his right
forearm. In letters that looked like they'd been written by a child,
it read, "BE PATIENT."

Curiosity got the better of me, and I had to follow him as
he went to stand in front of a shower. I pretended to shower
and stole a look at his other forearm. It was a little hard to read
because the tattoo was longer, but at last I saw why people in
the bathhouse wouldn't go near him. In equally clumsy writing,
the tattoo read, "BE NICE."

THE BLAZER

I WONDER IF there's anything more natural than reading the paper on the subway. Missing your stop because of that newspaper or leaping for the exit just before the doors close because of the same newspaper, are also natural things that happen. When these actions are repeated on a normal basis, one can be considered "obsessed with the newspaper," and I, too, am a newspaper addict. Like most people who are salaried office workers, I live in your average apartment complex and have to make a transfer on the subway to get to work.

On a spring day, especially if it's one that gives you a surprise preview of the heat of the summer, most office workers take their blazers off and carry them on their arms. That day, I, too, set out of the house carrying my blazer, and headed for the subway with the newspaper I'd bought at a newsstand, tucked underneath my arm.

As soon as I got on, I placed my blazer on the overhead rack. Since you can't have items falling out of your jacket, you need to take any items out of the pockets. So I took out my wallet and cigarettes and put them in my pants pocket. I placed my blazer on the rack, secured myself enough wiggle room as I opened my newspaper, and soon got lost in it. If I were to compare it to being submerged in water, I started with dark water at my ankles, which gradually reached my neck, until I only had a sliver of my senses above the water's surface, allowing me to hear the subway announcement

At some point, even though my auditory senses picked up the information that I had to get off to make my transfer, well, even though I'd heard it, I was a little late in processing all of the information. The moment I realized that I was late, I grabbed the blazer on the rack, folded my newspaper, and rushed toward the exit, pushing people aside. I transferred to another line, arrived at the office and began the day. Of course, before I started work, I hung my blazer on a hanger like all of the other workers in the office. I took out the items in the pocket of my pants and placed them in my desk drawer. My wallet, keys, cigarettes, and some loose change. I looked for my matches, but couldn't find them. Matches are easily replaceable so I decided not to spend more time looking for the ones I'd had. Lunchtime rolled around and I set out of the office with my colleagues.

There probably isn't anyone who'd think strangely of office workers holding their blazers on their arms, looking for a table during a busy lunch hour. I can't say whether it's necessary or not to take your jacket to a restaurant. That's a matter of personal habit. If on a personal level it's called a habit, on a societal level I think it's perhaps called a social norm?

"Hey Kim, is that a different blazer?"

The three or four of us were almost the same age, and we entered our company around the same time, got married around the same time, and had similar numbers of sons and daughters around the same time. It'd been quite a while since we called each other by our last names instead of our titles at the office or by our first names. Heeding what "Cho" said, I peered at my blazer. Sure enough, the color was a little different and so was the pattern of the cloth. My pants were gray, but the jacket was a deeper shade of gray with horizontal stripes.

"This isn't mine. I guess I took the wrong one from the office."

But there was no way. I never liked that kind of pattern, and there wasn't anybody who had that type of suit on in my part of the office. So it must've gotten switched. But where? By force of habit, I thought of my wallet and was relieved to discover that it was in my back pocket. When I felt around the pocket of the blazer in question, a wallet that was a bit bigger than my own came into my grasp. "Cho" showed no interest after pointing out that my blazer and pants were mismatched. I didn't mention it any further and had no intention of making myself look like an idiot and making a fuss over the wallet.

After lunch, I came back to my desk and took out the wallet. In it, there were two credit cards like any normal office worker's wallet, a driver's license, and a single receipt. The receipt was from a peculiar-sounding institution called "The Black Rose" and was a bill for a few hundred thousand won. On the driver's license was a guy with glasses like me, glaring at the camera in the subway station photo booth, where you could take and get your photo developed in less than five minutes. My wallet carried similar content. The only thing different about his wallet was the cleanliness and affluence indicated by a crisp one-hundred-dollar bill and the three or four hundred-thousand-won checks in it. There was a business card but the name on it was different from the one on the driver's license. I had his whole life figured out in an instant, and even caught a whiff of his past and future. Up until this point, all I'd done was take a look inside his wallet, without much thought. But when I found out that there was no business card to lead me to the owner of the blazer, I was incredibly torn, wanting to steal this man's identity and money. So I began to think about what kind of identity I could make with what I'd found in the pockets of my blazer. Matches! There were probably matches in my pocket. I imagined the puzzled face of a guy thinking about what clues a box of matches with a picture of a camel on it could provide. The guy would first try to wait. He'd try to recall whether he had his business card in his wallet. He'd also think about the level of ethics and morals in this country, and perhaps remember the teachers in his past who emphasized the importance of those things. He'd then imagine every bad thing possible about a person who carried nothing but a box of matches in his blazer, and, when he didn't get contacted by the guy, might tear up the match box, shove my blazer into a trash can, and kick the thing. Even though doing so wouldn't improve the situation. Hence I made a call to the person listed on the business card that was in the wallet. The man on the business card said he was a friend of the blazer's owner and I was easily able to find out the phone number of this man, who was probably awaiting a call.

The guy seemed confused. He may have still been thinking that the blazer he had with him was his own. Then perhaps he decided that there was still hope for the future of this land and this nation. That wasn't important. We agreed to meet. We decided that we'd each look for another guy holding a blazer on his arm in the middle of the street.

I'll let you imagine what happened next. One thing I'll tell you is that the guy gave me his business card as we parted. It had the phone number of the headquarters of a restaurant franchise on it. Once in a while, I stop to look at the card when I go through my Rolodex. Nobody deems it odd that I'm smiling as I look at a business card.

The moral of this story: If you find a wallet that's not yours, return it to its owner.

GLOBALIZATION

HE DRIVES A small vehicle, smaller than a truck but bigger than a sedan, and is a supplier of dry goods for bars. He picks up dried shrimp, anchovies, peanuts, bananas, thinly sliced beef or fish at the market, divides them into disposable cases and supplies them at double the cost of the materials. Included with the cost of materials is the labor of his wife and neighboring housewives who lead similar lives like his wife's. Hundreds of other costs such as shipping, car payment installments, electricity, water, parking tickets given to cars parked in front of the bars, cigarette money for the bouncers of the bars, etc., are also included in the price of the dried goods. Maybe this is what people refer to as the cost of sale without thinking about it too much. At the bar, the dry goods that he toiled over were sold at ten or twenty times the actual cost. So what was the pretext there? Men's cosmetics for the waiters, the dazzling lighting, cool music? Even a guy like him, who had a strange way of thinking, couldn't venture a guess. All he knew was that the excessive profit that came from selling the small plates of dry goods that he supplied wasn't being shared with the ladies who worked in the bars. Perhaps that was why those ladies didn't recommend the likes of small plates of dry food to customers. If they ever did make recommendations, it was probably the more expensive foods like packaged chestnuts, fresh fruit, ginseng, or side dishes like fish roe, which his strange mind wouldn't consider anyway. Accordingly, he never had to be friendly with the girls who worked at the bars and neither did he have to hand them any extra bills for cigarettes, as he did with the waiters-in-training. However, one of those girls was the reason his ligament got torn.

He was making a supply run at one of the underground saloons where hostesses entertain customers when he spotted a pretty hostess crying in the hallway. He was carrying a heavy load, so he told himself that she probably had a good reason for crying and passed by before one of his strange thoughts, which were his sole hobby and specialty, could come to mind. He saw her again on his way out. She was surrounded by a group of young guys who had a lot of gel in their hair, but she wasn't crying. The young guys were shouting at her with drunken slurs to cry. As he passed them by, he heard English cuss words like Sucking, Cock, Dick, and Fucking being repeated, in the middle of Seoul no less. Strangely enough, he was reminded of the KATUSAs he bumped into at church while he was a trainee during his military service. Although Korean citizens, the KATUSA soldiers wore the same uniforms as the American soldiers, their skin tone seemed light like the American soldiers and they said they'd be working on the American base. He remembered how envious he was of their being able to eat what American soldiers eat, talk in English like the American soldiers, and just generally have a better quality of military life, like the American soldiers did. Right before his strange thoughts brought him to the end of the hall, the girl slapped an especially young looking kid among the guys who resembled the KATUSAs. Like the minister's saying goes, "As you sow, so you shall reap." The girl was slapped by the other guys. Like the verse that states, "Your beginnings will seem humble so prosperous will your future be," she was slapped a dozen times before she fell to the ground, her nose bleeding. The kid who'd been slapped by the girl in the beginning had been rubbing his cheek in the corner before he stepped up to tromp on her luscious hair with his foot. The only people in the hall were the man, who was unable to decide whether to leave or stay and just kept rubbing his hands together as his strange thoughts continuously clouded his mind, and the people who were hitting each other. There wasn't a particular reason why he turned himself from them. What if he used his strange personality and asked the guys whether they were embarrassed about ganging up on one girl? Would they understand his fluent Korean? Would the bar owner, waiter, or customers later criticize him for crossing the line as a supplier? Wouldn't that kind of criticism lead to the end of his business with the bar? So he tried to think of other strange things to do that wouldn't cause such a misunderstanding. Should I go back to the kitchen at the other end of the hall pretending that I forgot something? Should I noisily march past them as if I were incredibly busy? If they became aware that there was another person in the hall, wouldn't they at least stop the hitting? What if they continued the hitting? I'll open the kitchen door and call out for a waiter I know. Oh, you know, I forgot to ask. When's the next time I collect the bill? That's what I'll ask. However the incident happened before he could execute any of these ideas, which were half-decent and half-strange.

When he recovered his senses at the police station, his forearm had been split open, looking a lot like a starting block on a running track, and a waiter was stating that somebody had taken his knife the minute he looked out of the kitchen, but he didn't get to look at the person's face. I guess for some reason that didn't allow her to come near a police station, the girl, who was also the victim, the concerned party, the contributor, and the much-needed witness, was nowhere to be seen. Neither were the kids who'd hit the girl. Actually, there was one he did see, and it was the guy who got slapped. In flowing English, the guy said he was a Korean-American with American citizenship, that he was assaulted (Oh my God!) while arguing with the lady over her demanding an excessive tip, that soon after he was slapped and kicked in the balls (A terrible beating!) by a bully who was standing by, that the people who were in the hallway with him were Koreans who'd helped him communicate, and that he'd never met them before. The police officers listened attentively to every word in the guy's English statement, and as if to show off to each other that they'd understood every word, they laughed loudly at some points in the account. They then exchanged opinions among themselves while they carefully translated the statement, before getting the guy's confirmation and putting it into a file. Incredibly, the police officer that was assigned to the supplier because of his lacking English skills gravely said, "You must be a pimp who exploits poor girls working at bars. Well, you're in for it today." He went on to interrogate him Korean-style, banging the desk with his hand. While this dragged on, his ligament injury, which needed emergency treatment, was eating up his forearm. He was in such pain while the others were carrying on with their strange thoughts and actions that he wasn't able to do what he did best. Even after he was driven to the emergency room, he had no way of getting compensation from either the one who wielded the knife, the one who was slapped, the girl, the owner of the bar, the waiter, or the police officer. They all did what they had to do and were done with their business.

That evening, the president was on television saying that globalization was the only way for us to survive. It was the two-thousandth time that the president had mentioned the word globalization on television. A police officer on night duty made a note in his notebook—"Globalization is the only way for us to survive."

O

IN THE MILITARY, there are wonderful words that are only used there. I'm about to introduce to you a memorable idiom among them. All soldiers can increase their combat power through self-reflection. When a soldier is self-reflecting, it must be done seriously and thoroughly, in military style. An expression that conveys such implications is "Grab one's O and self-reflect," with the word O meaning a male's genitals. For your information, if we compared the world of military speech to kimchi stew or walnut pastry or the desert, the word O would be the kimchi in kimchi stew, the walnut in the walnut pastry, and the oasis in the desert. The following is the story about how the expression came to be.

The expression originated in a training corps for officers. The drill sergeant wasn't an officer. Maybe that was the reason, but the military cadets just weren't obeying his orders. After much contemplation, the drill sergeant made the cadets undress and go out to the training ground in the rain. He then made each cadet grab the O of the person in front of him and run around the track in a single file line. (There's also the expression "the military is all about lines.") That was the first time such a bizarre sight took place, the first since mankind was put on earth. That was when the phrase, "Grab one's O and self-reflect" was coined.

Well, no. There's also a theory that the expression had already existed, but it was carried out for the first time on that occasion. Just bear in mind that the O here is not to be one's own, but someone else's.

THE AMUSING LIFE - 4
On Exercise

SINCE MY EARLY, impoverished days until now, there haven't been many sports that I haven't tried. The forms of exercise I'd recommend to a person who doesn't have the time and money to invest in exercising is breathing, walking, stretching, running, etc. If you do have a bit of money, I'd recommend something like tennis, which requires brand-name tennis shoes, clothes, rackets and such. In my twenties, I usually stuck to breathing and stretching, and only when I entered my thirties was I able to take some interest in tennis. Of course, all of these are excellent forms of exercise that many people enjoy.

If you do have some money to spare, want to feel more special than others, and are looking for a sport to take up, I recommend golf. It costs you a substantial amount of money to play golf in Korea. Golf clubs, booking fees, tips, etc., all cost money, and you should be ready to pay extra if you're eating at a clubhouse, as even a bowl of ox bone soup costs double or triple what it costs in a regular restaurant. A sport on a similar level to golf would be hunting. Hunting is a seasonal sport enjoyed in the winter, and there's a limit to the amount of game you can hunt. Also, the hunting grounds open in one or two alternating provinces every year, so the sport does feel a bit laborious. Anyway, if you're at a level of enjoying golf or hunting, you are at about the same level as I was in my early forties. Oh, and, hunting isn't child's play so you do need to have a rifle, breed a few dogs, and also have a Jeep with good performance features—if it's all the same, a gasoline Jeep with at least a 3,000 cc engine is recommended—so it'll cost you money here and there.

If these costs mean nothing to you, if you're a person who can say that that kind of cost is peanuts when it comes to maintaining your health through exercise, enjoying life, and ultimately improving yourself, and if you are a person who is looking for something completely different, I recommend horseback riding. If you already enjoy horseback riding as a hobby, you're probably one of the considerably rich in Korea, as I'd been in my late forties. If you're sick of getting up early in the morning, the fresh air in the grassy plains, the soft and warm texture of a horse's back, and horse manure, I'd like to recommend yachting. You control your own schedule on a yacht, whether it's swimming, fishing, cooking, tanning, etc. A yacht is a floating castle. You're the lord of that castle. Something that's comparable to yachting is light-sport aircraft flying, which is enjoyed by people like my friend Herbert von Karajan. I'm not sure if you can say yachting or flying a light-sport aircraft are forms of exercise. The apparatus is responsible for too much of the activity. So if you don't want to take up something that seems questionable as a sport, what sport could be more physical, special, and fitting for one of the richest men in the world like yourself? It's polo, a sport I'm deeply absorbed in these days.

Polo is a game where players on horseback use a wooden stick called a mallet and horse hooves to roll a ball into the opponent's goal. There's no man who won't clench his fists with adrenaline when he hears the powerful galloping of heavily breathing men and horses, the petal-like sparks set off by horse hooves on the dusty plains, and the smacking of mallets like a pair of sparring bucks. Despite the sweating and shouting, it's indeed a gentleman's game, and truly a game for heroes, as there is the thrilling joy of victory. If you're to play, you first need a playing field, for which a grass field with an approximate area of 300 yards (275 meters) x 250 yards (183 meters) will do. Playing time is eight rounds of seven-and-a-half minute segments, with three minutes in between rounds. Each goal is worth one point, but there's a strict and unusual rule that takes away half of the points you've earned if you commit a foul.

If you wish to enjoy polo, you must have three or four horses ready to go at all times. For that, you'll need a stable, an animal trainer, manager, and a grassy plain where the horses can practice. Oh yes, you'll also need a meadow. Wait, I forgot the horse bath and a restroom for the horses, because good breeds only relieve themselves in designated areas. Horses used in polo are called polo ponies. It's extremely difficult to obtain highbred polo ponies, a problem that's giving me a headache these days as well. Ah, last but not least, since polo is a multiplayer sport, you must have several friends who are rich and enjoy sports. No need to worry about the money it'll cost you, since you, like me, are probably as rich as a medieval lord.

Life is short and the grasses of May are thus youthful and beautiful. Let's play a game some time.

THE HANGOVER REMEDY

HAVING SET OUT thirty minutes earlier than usual, Ryu buys the paper from the newsstand next to the bus stop and lights a cigarette. One minute during rush hour is equivalent to thirty minutes in any other part of the day, and he still has thirty of those single minutes left. If it were any other day, he'd be desperately trying to open his sleepy eyes as he trudges toward the bathroom, like a cow being dragged to a slaughterhouse. But today's version of him is different from yesterday's version.

"Start the day thirty minutes early and come back home an hour early," he solemnly promised his colleagues and family at work and at home. It's a weary life, barely sliding into the office in time to hear the ring of the starting bell in the morning, pouring after-work drinks down your throat in the name of taking the edge off of a stressful day, and then barely sliding into one's home before the clock strikes midnight. Why do we waste life like this? I'm over it.

Here comes the multi-seat bus. But he figures he has some time today. He wasn't done with his cigarette. I can let one bus go. Heck, I still have plenty of time. The multi-seat bus stops and a few smartly-dressed people climb on. The bus doesn't leave right away but lingers for the model citizens who start and end their day a little bit earlier.

Ryu takes another drag of his cigarette and looks at the people asleep on the quiet bus. He, too, can now live an exemplary life. If he gets on the bus now, he can sit the entire way and probably take a nap until he gets to the office. But how can he help it if sometimes a drag of smoke feels more precious than thirty minutes of sleep? After the bus leaves, Ryu puts out his cigarette, wraps the butt in a gum wrapper, and puts it in his pocket, like the exemplary citizen that he is. Even after that, he has twenty of those single minutes left.

The bus comes but Ryu doesn't get on. He couldn't see any empty seats. Doesn't an exemplary citizen who started the day off earlier than others deserve at least a seat on the bus? There'll be more buses, so heck, he'll wait a little longer.

A few minutes pass and another multi-seat bus arrives. But the people who are standing nearer to the bus rush toward it, and it doesn't seem likely that there would be any seats left for him, since he was late, trying to fold his newspaper. He ponders for a minute. What's a multi-seat bus without any available seats? I'm an exemplary citizen, and I have my pride. I can't ride a multi-seat bus without an available seat. He thinks to himself that he still has over ten minutes.

After the multi-seat bus leaves, he neatly folds the newspaper and takes his position at the edge of the pavement. But the long-awaited multi-seat bus doesn't show up. He gets the uneasy feeling that he might have to fight his way through the crowd to ride the bus, like any other day, despite having arrived thirty minutes earlier. No way, I still have five good minutes. But there are no more multi-seat buses. Only a string of regular buses. And even those are getting more crowded. He thinks about getting on a regular bus. When he thinks about the extra thirty minutes he had, it seems unfair. Forget about taking a leisurely ride on a multi-seat bus, how could he share a bus with the low-lives who still reek of the alcohol they consumed last night and probably ran helter-skelter to catch the regular bus?

However, his precious time keeps ticking away. More people are trying to get a taxi. He decides to wait for the multi-seat bus, even if it means, worst-case scenario, he'll have to catch a cab.

Just before his last golden five minutes are up, the multi-seat bus arrives. But as usual, the one that comes around this time is so crowded that there's barely enough room to stand. He can't stand how unfair it is that he has to go through the same hassle even though he left the house thirty minutes early. He brazenly passes up the multi-seat bus and heads toward the taxi stand. It'll cost him more, but he has no other choice, when he thinks about how he started out early. He reminds himself that money isn't everything. It's clear that he must make a habit of getting out of the house earlier. But if he barely slid into his office chair on the dot, just like yesterday, what would he have to look forward to by leaving the house early?

There aren't many people who ride a taxi around that time. Taxis are your last resort when you aren't going to make it on time, even on a regular bus. He does the math inside the taxi. In his wallet, he had a 10,000 won bill and a 1,000 won bill, just in case he took a multi-seat bus. He opened up his newspaper again. The ride was swift, except for when the driver stopped to pick up one other person going in the same direction. The woman who shared the cab got off before him and handed the driver a 10,000 won bill.

"Don't you have change?"

The woman shook her head. The driver, who looked like a man of some age, then turned to him.

"Do you?"

"All I have is a 10,000-won."

At this, the driver licks his lips as he counts the change in 1,000-won bills and hands it to the woman.

"What are we going to do? I don't have change. There isn't any place to get any change at rush hour."

Ryu remembers that there's a pharmacy he often goes to near his stop, and thinks he can get some change there. As soon as the taxi stops, he asks the driver to wait as he hurriedly runs into the pharmacy.

"I'm so sorry, but could you give me something to buy so I can get some change . . .?"

The pharmacist, who was reading the paper, looks up at him, nods, and reaches for a pack of medicine with a liquid supplement to wash it down. While the pharmacist counts the change, Ryu dumps the powder into his mouth out of habit. After paying the taxi driver, he crosses the overpass and heads toward his office.

His troubles pay off. He arrives at least twenty minutes earlier than usual. He enjoys the early morning calmness of the office as he waits for his colleague, who'll slide into the office barely on time, still hungover and bloated from the previous night's drinking. His head feels clear. In this condition, he could work all day without stress. The taxi fare was worth every penny.

Yet as time passes Ryu starts to feel funny. His head feels so clear and wide-awake that it feels like he's floating. Little things bother him and he reacts to even the smallest sound. It's almost lunchtime when he realizes why this is happening. The medicine he took at the pharmacy was his usual hangover cure.

EL DORADO

IT HAPPENED IN a far distant past, long before people followed nature's law of being born from dust and returning to dust. Back then, the ions, which were unstable because of the lightning bolts striking billions of times a day in an atmosphere that was sticky as mud, busily searched for a partner to form new molecular structures. In a time when it was impossible for plant and animal life to survive, the only intelligent life-forms were the golden giants of El Dorado. They lived in a golden cave up on the top of a mountain because this place was the source of their food, and thus of their bodies and their excrement. These giants consumed, digested, and excreted gold, but at the same time dreamed of sleeping on a pillow of gold and giving birth to golden children. In the golden age of El Dorado, nobody thought of eating gold that was spread on the floor, and thus nobody fought over gold, either.

In the unending passage of time, the excrement that fell from their bodies rolled out of the cave and flowed downward and away in accordance with the laws of gravity. And from a certain point on, the giants had no choice but to eat low-quality gold. After even more time passed, finally they went against the law of nature, which said, "All that glitters is not gold," and ate everything that glittered whether it was dew on a spider web or brass.

Thanks to this, the gold that made up their bodies became more impure, and their impure bodies produced impure thinking and their impure thinking wasn't able to tell the difference between pure gold and impure gold. Most of them had indigestion and slept on less rich pillows of gold. They'd say they missed the old days in their sleep. Not too long after, a giant who was discovered eating his own excrement shocked their society. There were criticisms voiced, but only by older giants. More and more of the younger generation wanted instant gratification instead of the virtues of self-control and ethics that characterized intelligent beings. Finally, it came to the point where consuming one's excrement in private was considered the same as excreting in private.

Eventually, war broke out among them. A heated debate arose regarding a giant who ended up exposing the layer of dirt underneath the gold when he dug up and ate the golden floor of the cave, which was the giants' home and cradle. People were divided into groups that insisted either that "Continuing life is of more importance than preserving or maintaining the roof or walls," or that "It's better to die clean and with dignity than to continue life by consuming even the floor of our cave, which is the protoplasm of our existence and the shell that will nurse our descendants." The argument led to a fight that caused members of the species to kill and be killed by one another. It doesn't matter which side won. The winners chewed off the meat of the losers' bodies. None of the giants called this cruel or shameful. They knew that if they said such a thing they'd also immediately be devoured by the others. Time passed and they ran out of those enemies as well. Giants who were once on the same side were split up into two sides, four sides, and eight sides, but the lesson of the previous war prevented them from recklessly starting another war. They tried to find a more reasonable way to eat each other. The solution was this: they'd decide on a victim by drawing straws, and the assailant would bring back an arm or leg of the victim. They'd then draw straws again to decide the order in which they'd eat. They each had dozens of what were similar to human arms, so drawing straws was a reliable way to ensure peace for a certain period of time. It also fulfilled the role of awakening the senses to games and helping them forget about the times, which were filled with misery. Suddenly, bluish, impure patterns appeared on their bodies. This impurity, which was later named copper by humans, had spread like a disease among the weakened bodies of the giants.

Another extensive period of time had passed. The giants were merely living day to day, battling their hunger and fear. The spots on their bodies grew larger and larger, and in the unseen inner corners of their bodies were a growing number of various metals that glittered but weren't gold, for example, silver, white gold, lead, mercury, cadmium, and copper. One day the golden giants reached the agreement that it was impossible to maintain the purity of the tribe and its society any longer. They made an important decision. They selected one giant to leave in search of a new El Dorado. This giant was given a set of arms and legs that were of high purity. The selected one left, shedding golden tears, and those who were left behind, stayed. The giants who were left moved as little as possible and waited for their dispatched envoy and explorer to return with good news. However, he never came back. They gathered their hopes once more and selected a new envoy. He left. No tears were shed this time. He also didn't return. They continued to send more. There were fewer arms and legs to send them off with, and at some point they realized that they had no more arms or legs to give.

Some more time passed. Most of them ended up dying and the golden age of the golden giants came to an end. However, there was a final survivor, a clever giant who was especially patient and strong enough to outlast his hunger. He's the last golden giant to be recorded in human history.

After all the other giants had passed away, he was able to survive longer than the entire span of existence of his kind by eating the dead bodies. Yet he was no exception to the harshness of time. He could starve or maybe fool himself into thinking he ate for a year or two, but he couldn't fool himself or skip eating for one or two billion years. In the end, he had no choice but to start eating himself. He started with the fingernails, then the toenails and the hair, things that didn't involve too much guilt. He shed tears of gold and licked them with his tongue while he ate his own golden fingers and golden toes. This bought him another twenty million years. Next, he went on to his foot. He was sustained another thirty thousand years. He ate his left shin and then grabbed his right shin. Twenty thousand years passed by. The reason only twenty thousand years passed even though he'd consumed something as large as his shin was that as he started to self-consume, the level of his purity rapidly declined.

When the ancestors of humankind first appeared at the far-removed lower part of the stream, all that was left of the giant was part of his chest, digestive organs, neck, and face. Because he'd carelessly eaten his arms early on, he couldn't eat the body parts that couldn't be reached with his mouth. In the very last moment of his life, the final end of the exalted golden giants, just when the voices of humans started to be heard from far away, his mouth and throat were hideously flipped inside out in an effort to swallow itself. He ripped out his tongue and gnawed at his own teeth. He died full of remorse that he didn't get to his ear when he'd had the chance.

The first human to visit El Dorado put his stone axe down and stood mesmerized in front of the shimmering lump of gold.

He'd traveled upstream following the glowing object. Finally, he brought his friends.

Much later, a statue topped by a golden head was erected on the far distant top of the mountain. Its torso was made of bronze, below that was iron, and the feet were made of the same substance as the ground on which it stood.

THE STORY OF ↑ AND ↓

ABOUT THIRTY YEARS ago, there was a teacher who was called the "demented dog" by his elementary school students. He unfailingly carried around a large, coarse club that went with his sizable physique and rugged muscles. He wielded it whenever and wherever, and he was well-known for spewing out foul language, which he didn't allow his students to use. It looked like he enjoyed such behavior naturally, and he was proud that students feared him.

The name of the student is ↑. ↑ was an introvert who mostly stayed in the background and had never gotten rabies. When he became a 6th grader, ↓ joined his class on an overnight field trip. Right before the bus hit the road, the demented dog made his rounds of the buses, hitting, knuckling, and cursing, claiming to establish military-style discipline with a non-military group of students. As always, ↑ went unnoticed by the demented dog. That's not to say that he had a good time just because he wasn't noticed. Everybody had to crawl under their seats when the demented dog yelled, "Grenades above the seats!" and when he yelled, "Full bus!" students had to throw themselves toward the back of the bus so hard that they felt that parts of their body would burst. Later in life, ↑ would go through the same type of training in the military, but there military discipline was necessary, and perhaps falling grenades from above were an actual danger. The first time he was put through such training in his life, ↑ was a child in elementary school. He says that was the first time ↑ ever vowed revenge. The bus briefly stopped in Busan, passed through the industrial complex in Ulsan and arrived in Gyeongju. At the lodge, two teachers were given one room to share whereas the students, who were smaller than the teachers, were given one room to share with fourteen other students. He recalls that the sizes of the rooms were the same. The demented dog, who brought along his club on the field trip, was specially given a room to himself, or to be more precise, he assigned it to himself because none of the students or teachers wished to share a room with the demented dog. That's how ↑ ended up sleeping in a room with fourteen other kids. ↑ says he vowed revenge one more time. The students had a dinner of rice with nothing but salty, spicy kimchi and inedible anchovies, which were as big as their fingers (following the demented dog's instructions to eat quietly and thankfully), while the teachers enjoyed a grand feast with drinks on the side. The students were ordered by the demented dog to go to sleep as soon as they'd eaten. Yet the room was so cramped that it was impossible to sleep lying down, unless students slept on top of each other. Once more, ↑ vowed revenge. Because he clenched his entire body doing so, he suddenly needed to go to the restroom. On the way to the restroom, ↑ caught sight of the demented dog, who had fallen asleep drunk, with his door open. The restroom was, of course, the conventional kind, dirty and dark. There, ↑ says he found a matchstick. Following an instinct that he himself couldn't understand, he smudged a little bit of the special product of the restroom that was in a ↑-shaped pile on the tip of the matchstick. ↑ exited the restroom and stood before the demented dog. With lightning speed, which he couldn't comprehend even later on, he put the tip of the matchstick under the demented dog's nose. The demented dog's hand initially wiped the spot where the matchstick touched, and he then continued to pick his nose several times with his thick finger, before turning around and carrying on with his snoring.

The next morning, the students washed their faces in a single file line, used one towel to wipe fifteen faces, and like the previous day, got back in line to walk toward the large hall where breakfast was prepared. The teachers were already seated at the tables, and only the demented dog was worked up and yelling as usual. The students sat down in a neat line and picked up their spoons in unison, as they were ordered to. But then, the demented dog, who was supposed to yell, "Begin your meal!" tilted his head from side to side and questioned the child sitting directly across him.

"You farted, didn't you?"

The color drained from the child's face as he shook his head. The demented dog tilted his head once again and asked the kid sitting next to him, "Was it you?"

The kid shook his head and his face turned blue as well. The demented dog glared at the kids, and then, shaking his head, said, "Begin your meal," and returned to his seat. He reached for his spoon, but instead asked his colleague who was busily shoveling food into his mouth, "Did somebody fart?"

Everybody shook their heads. Tilting his head in confusion, he started to eat. From then on, all the way home, he continued to tilt his head and repeatedly ask, "You farted, didn't you?"

"Is it you?"

"Who farted?"

A LETTER TO A POET

THE CRY OF the magpie accompanied the arrival of a letter. The envelope alone, with a luxurious, golden design on it, looks like it would cost more than our mailbox. The paper inside the envelope is also thick and fancy like parchment. Anyway, the content of the letter can be summarized as follows.

The operational board of directors of the Special Fund for Worldwide Poetry Promotion is deeply concerned with the global rise of frivolous cultural media that wears a mask of novelty, as well as the decline in the number of people who write, read, recite, and enjoy true poetry due to commercialism, and has been forced to endure not only regret but outrage at how this phenomenon is erasing the glory and dignity of poetry, and hereby aims to take special action to allow citizens of the world to experience and to praise the brilliance and beauty of true poetry once again. Already, countless poets around the world have expressed full support for our proposal. In Korea, all of the winners of the many poetic literature awards from the 1980s to 2006, including the poet Kim Hyul-Geun, the first Korean to receive the Nobel Prize in literature in 2006, are included in this group.

You've been recommended to the board by our Korean branch, which noted the fact that you're a full-time poet who has, with little interest in awards or fame, continuously written sophisticated poetry in twenty books of poems since your debut, despite all kinds of difficulties. Every member of the board has been consulted about reaching the following conditions.

1. As soon as the consent of poet Song Okze is confirmed, the board will immediately provide a lifetime subsidy of one hundred million won in a lump sum.

1. Poet Song Okze is to delegate all rights and duties regarding all future poems to the board, and discontinue all official and personal poetry writing. If this condition is violated, Song must pay a penalty of fifty billion won per poem to the board.

1. The board will secretly commission poems from distinguished poets of the world and strictly seal and store them. None of these poems will be introduced until this corrupt world begs for the restoration of true poetry.

1. Please send us your agreement to this proposal in the enclosed return envelope immediately.

PS. This proposal will automatically incinerate in an hour.

"Who are these lunatics?"

Startled at my rage, my wife peers out from the room where she was patching up a hole in our child's sock. She looks even paler than usual. I am suddenly reminded of the promise I made her three months before to get her some iron supplements.

"What is it, honey?"

I place the letter in my wife's coarse hands. My wife turns toward the window that was broken three years ago by our kids and starts reading. There's no denying it's winter. The floors, stripped of their warmth, are as cold as broken glass.

"What does it mean, that it'll automatically incinerate?"

"They must be joking. Too many movies. If they gave me the money that it costs to install that kind of device, we wouldn't have to worry about eating for two weeks."

Without warning, the letter that was in my wife's grasp let out a flash-like sound, "Poof!" and immolated itself in the blink of an eye.

"Dear!"

My wife's fingers turned black, but thankfully they didn't seem burned. As she came back to her senses, she mumbled in a frail voice, "I don't think they're kidding." The letter was burned, but the return envelope dropped to the ground without so much as a speck of dust on it.

"I ought to kill them."

I pick up the return envelope and try tearing it with all my might. But it doesn't rip. I run to the kitchen and place the envelope on the stove. But it's been three days since the gas was cut off. I madly fumble around for scissors and matches. My wife quietly comes to me and holds my hand.

"I'm fine, honey."

"What should we do with these crazy bastards?"

"Do as you wish. That's what you've always done."

The sun is setting in our silence. In the end, I pick up the crumpled letter. I'm unable to tell her not to carefully pick up and smooth out the return envelope as she does.

THE SHOES

THERE WAS A poor fellow who lived hand-to-mouth. One rainy day, he was dragging his tired feet home. He abruptly stopped in front of the shoe store he passed by every day. A pair of black shoes on one side of the shelf caught his eye. The shoes on the shelf looked light and sturdy, made of good quality leather. He glanced at his tattered shoes, which water seeped into, and then back at the shoes in the window. He felt especially lonely that night. The shoes, shimmering under the bright store lights, floated before his eyes as he lay curled up in his small room, damp and lightless as his own future.

The next morning, he stopped by the shoe store to take another look at the shoes before going to work. He'd stop by to look at the shoes even on days when he was lucky enough to earn some money and carry home firewood or a sack of rice he'd bought with it. He went to see the shoes every day, twice a day for dozens of days, never missing one.

As usual, he was looking at the shoes, which now felt as familiar as a friend. The door of the shoe store opened and the owner walked out.

"Excuse me, what do you do there every day?"

He took a step back, with his face already red like a guilty person.

"You've been coming to my window for months now. I want to know why."

He stammered, "I came to look at the shoes. Just to look. I'm sorry."

The shop owner stood straight with his belly out as he said, "I don't charge for looking. Why don't you come in and look at them all you want."

While he hesitated, the shop owner urged him into the store. The inside of the store was as warm as a part of his childhood. The owner took the shoes from the shelf.

"I made these myself, but they're an excellent pair of shoes. Try them on. You don't have to pay to just try them on."

He carefully slipped into them. The shoes fit as if they were custom-made for him. The owner said to him, "It's like you were born to own these shoes. Would you like to buy them?"

In a ruthful tone, he told him that he had no money, and that he was a person who lived from hand to mouth. The owner stared at him.

"I have my pride. Pride as a shoemaker, and as a merchant. If you truly refuse to buy these shoes, I plan to remove them from the shelf."

The shoes were the only flicker of hope that lit up his heart for a long time. He stood there at a loss for words. The shop owner asked him how much money he had. He said if he added up everything he had, it wouldn't amount to one-fourth of what was on the price tag.

"These past few years, I've never seen another person look at my shoes with such adoration as you do. It doesn't matter if you don't have enough money, you can have the shoes. Don't take it the wrong way. I'm not doing this because I pity you. I just love that the shoes I made are going into the hands of their rightful owner."

The shop owner put his old shoes in a new box and he gave the owner of the shoe shop every last coin he had. Walking out in his new shoes, he felt so happy he thought he'd float away.

Time passed. The shoes were sturdy, but because they were the only pair that he wore, the soles got worn out. He went to the store where he'd bought the shoes to get his soles replaced. The owner replaced the soles for free. A couple of years later, his soles got worn out again. He went to the shoe store again. Trends had changed, so it wasn't easy to find a sole that fit the shoes exactly, but the owner did everything he could to find a fitting sole to replace the old ones. There was a pleased smile on the shop owner's face as he refused to accept any payment. As he walked out of the store, an extra pair of soles in hand, he strangely did not feel as happy as the shop owner. He says a thought came to mind.

"Several more of these new soles, and my life will be over."

When he arrived home, he took the shoes off and placed them in the shoebox the shop owner had given him. He took out the old pair of shoes that were in them and ran out the door to look for work. He worked and worked until his shoes were completely tattered and torn. After that, he bought a new pair of shoes, paying for them in full with the money he'd earned.

Twenty years later, he still holds on to the special pair of shoes as if they were a brand-new pair. Along with the extra soles. Besides that pair he now has twenty more pairs of shoes. Those shoes are placed in a special glass cabinet with lights, which stands in the middle of the living room of his mansion, where his butler cares for them every day. Of course, the shoes on the highest, brightest shelf are that one special pair. Every time he looks at them, he feels like he's renewed.

CHRISTMAS TREES

IT MAY HAVE been ten years ago, maybe more, maybe less. I don't remember exactly how many years ago it was, but I remember the exact day. December 24th. I don't recall why, but I was on Jeju Island (Then again, I don't know what I'm doing here now either). I was alone and still hungover from drinking the night before. At a bar the previous night, I befriended the head of a gang, who'd just gotten out from jail, and completely plastered, I ended up in a nearby motel. The next morning, December 24th that is, I felt depressed. I was hungry but couldn't eat anything because I felt so nauseous I would've vomited up anything I ate. It seemed like I'd hit one of the lowest points of my life.

I fished out everything I had in my pockets and bought a mandarin, a special fruit of the island, and took the first bus that came into sight. After a while, Mt. Halla came into view (Then again, Mt. Halla comes into view wherever you are on Jeju Island). I got off at a place called Uhrimok Lodge. The only things you could see were the souvenir shop, a residence for the mountain rescuers, and a ticket window, and I was the only person in sight. Playing around with the mandarin in my pocket, I loitered about, poking my head in here and there. Just like a goose without purpose. Thanks to doing so, I came across some information. For instance, in the winter, the hiking trail was closed, yet the ticket window was still selling tickets, but naturally nobody was buying the tickets, etc. Then again I'd never bought a ticket to enter a national park at one of its ticket booths before. No matter what it took, I'd find a burrow to get into the mountains. The national parks of Mt. Jiri and Mt. Seorak have all been my victims. I went around the ticket booth, headed toward the stream, and set foot on Mt. Halla by way of a burrow dug by people like me who scoffed at the workers of the National Park Maintenance Office. The mountain was quiet. The winter and the mountain stood smothered together in silence.

Signs like "Trail Closed" and "Do Not Enter" continued to pass me by above my head, in the middle of the path, or on a rope. I continued to proceed. All I planned to do was get a small taste of feeling empty, of sweat, and of adventure. And if I could add to that, maybe a drag of a cigarette. Cautionary signs had nothing to do with people like me, who only pursued the trivial. I was donning a heavy wool coat with dress shoes, so it wasn't likely that anybody was going to take me for a hiker. I made it about two hundred meters, walking a little, then stopping a little, and so on, before sitting down on a rock. I took out a cigarette and lit it. I'd barely let out one puff of smoke when I heard whistle sounds coming from downhill. Soon enough red caps began to appear among the tree branches. They were likely a group of mountain rescuers, or control station workers, or policemen, or commandos who are also part of a special enforcement unit that chased down people like me, entering through burrows just to hike for free. Alarmed, I put out my cigarette and made a run for it uphill. Whoever they were in the red hats, I knew they meant bad news for me. The red hats kept on my tail, blowing on their whistles every now and then. I had no choice but to keep climbing. There was only one path.

I sped by the 1,300-meter mark like an arrow. I panted my way past the 1,350-meter mark. I was trying to catch my breath when I passed the 1,400-meter sign. The red hats were remarkably fast. I had to be faster. When I was near the 1,500-meter ridge, there was a sign that read Garden of Hurray. I considered surrendering by putting my arms up as if to shout hurray and just fall into the arms of those pesky pursuers. But surely they were more than annoyed with me at this point, plus I'd have to fork over at least the entrance fee to this national park and I had no money. Plus, sitting down to think these thoughts, my sweaty body was starting to shiver, so I ran and ran again.

When I reached the 1,700-meter point, there was a sign that indicated a shelter. I hid myself in the shelter. In front of it were college students in colorful sportswear rolling on the ground, undergoing physical training. Someone said they were replacing the hike with training because it was too dangerous for even an expedition team to climb any further. I slipped in among them and looked out at the mountain range with my arms crossed, trying my best to look as if I were one of them. The red hats arrived. They spoke with the ranger at the shelter and looked around. They looked at me, then away, and looked again several times, while I desperately disguised myself as a member of the climbing party, as part of the family, as one of the chiefs. While they were looking puzzled, I made my way to the back of the lodge. I took my cigarette out but didn't even think of lighting it. I just kept thinking this wasn't going to work. There I decided whether it would be up or down. I made a powerful spurt with my non-running shoes.

I ran as fast as I could for about a hundred meters and dove into the forest. I could hear the whistles again. I thought I could hear things like "Stop! You better stop!" It was the path that was too dangerous even for an expedition team, but I had to bite the bullet. I ran like a gusty wind, like a speedy boar. It wasn't long before I was standing in front of the metal ladder that led to the very top of the mountain. As expected, there were intimidating signs that read, "Off Limits" and "Hike Trail Closed" hanging next to icicles. Without any hesitation, I threw myself onto the ladder. I had barely climbed three or four steps when I felt the cutting wind lashing at the ladder and my body, and my palms stuck fast to the metal. I desperately climbed and climbed. I nearly died and also nearly lived. The red hats shouted something at the bottom of the ladder, but having seemed to decide that they couldn't chase me up the ladder, they shook their heads and disappeared into the woods. In an unexpected moment, the summit unveiled itself before my eyes.

The nation's sacred mountain, Mt. Halla. There, at 1,950 meters, I stood alone. In that moment, I felt no envy for even Sir Edmund Hillary, who'd climbed Mt. Everest. It was a climb without any supply of oxygen, without any equipment, and without any planning. Relishing the moment, I lit up the cigarette I'd been saving. When I finished the cigarette, I suddenly had nothing left to do. So I lit up another, and then another. Later, I lit up two cigarettes at once and puffed smoke out like I was a steam train. Even then I couldn't think of what to do. I was standing in a spot I'd come up to by my own will, but couldn't go back down the same way. That's what it's like at the top. That's how it is.

"Sir, what on earth are you doing here?"

The sight of the red hats felt like salvation. They said they'd taken the long route around the south wall where there was sunlight. I followed them down. Just as I'd predicted, they were mountain rescuers who were also combat police officers.

"I'm sorry I dragged you all the way up here."

They said it was okay. They actually thanked me. They were happy because they'd be granted a furlough for saving a distressed hiker. They didn't demand I pay the entrance fee, nor did they curse at me.

I saw trees hurray in the Garden of Hurray. The snow carried by the wind onto the branches was starting to ice up. When I gave the tree a gentle nudge, silver sparkles sprinkled down in the setting sunlight. Trees over here, trees over there, trees, trees, trees, trees, trees. They looked like a troop of Christmas trees. It was a forest of Christmas trees.

> When I was little, the Christmas tree was tall
> When we were in love, the other kids were playing
> Do not ask me why those times have passed away
> Nor why others had to go so far away

I sang that song at the top of my lungs, drinking soju and playing a broken guitar at the rescue ranger's residence that evening. That was how I spent Christmas Eve that year. I think it was ten years ago, maybe more or maybe less. But I do remember the day. It was December 24th.

THE FINAL MEANING
OF FEW WORDS

THE WATERS ARE ascending up the river. The sea's boiling. The ground can't stop shaking. The air smells like ashes. The sun looks dotted, like what a freckled eyeball would look like. "Could it be a nuclear war? An earthquake? A clash of meteorites?" people asked when it first happened. Nobody had any answers. When the first flash occurred, everything came to a halt. Gas, water, electricity, roads, streams, wind, time, history, everything stopped in its tracks. Things that were standing were pushed down and things that were lying down sprang up as if it were now time to do so. You can no longer see the people who moved like a huge pile of mud being washed away. The loudspeaker blaring out the importance of obeying rules can no longer be heard. The kids who cried and searched for their parents are also gone. The only people left are those who can't move. They're people whose legs were crushed under a building, who lost an eye, who didn't know where to go, or who believed that they couldn't just blindly follow where others were going. There are more. They're the people who can't leave because of something more important than their own lives.

There's a small head nestled under my armpit. Black and shiny hair, which is still the way it was when she was fifteen, or when she was twenty. The forehead that had such a hold on me when its smooth, eggshell-like surface would crinkle once in a while. That same forehead now shows traces of thin wrinkles. And the eyes. The border between the black and the white as vivid as in a girl's eyes. Can eyes smile? I wouldn't have believed it before, but now I do. You're able to express a smile without the help of the surrounding skin, just with the eyes. Under those eyes, a small yet long nose flares gently. Her mouth moves. At first it sounds like little puffs of wind, which cluster together in the air to become the vocal sounds of people. Isn't it almost the end? I put a finger to her small red lips. I think we'll be okay for a few hours. She moves her chapped lips, on which her lipstick no longer goes on smoothly. That long? She gives her legs a long stretch. That's not long. I wasted decades of my life for this moment, right now. She laughs out loud. You were always full of complaints, and so you are to the end. I can hear the sound of engines, like panting. Maybe I was mistaken, horses neighing. Dogs barking. Where did they all go? With every bit of strength I have, I wrap myself around her body like a vine, like a snake. Never mind that. Just think about us. She grimaces. I suddenly had a thought. Is this the end of the world, too? I pat her shoulders. But I'm happy. Her body is still warm. I hope my body feels the same to her. Our surroundings are just the right amount of dark and lukewarm. We lie facing each other like we did that time, long ago.

It's good to save it for last. That's how we have lived life as humans, missing each other more, fretting for each other more. If we'd finished everything we could possibly have done between us, if we'd completed everything we could in this life back then, what would've happened? We probably wouldn't have had reason to meet like this. We wouldn't have been this happy.

Stop talking. You're wasting time. She slightly tugs me toward her. I know that that's the sum of all the strength left in her. She starts to smell like a tree. My senses come alive like those of an insect. It gets more and more intense. What now? I pull her toward me. Do this. She crinkles her forehead as she smiles. You mean like this? And then before I can answer, she stops my mouth with her lips. This is what never happened in the past. Three minutes. Saliva, sweet like fruit juice, overflows my mouth. Forty seconds. A sharp and exquisite lightning with just the right amount of intensity passes through us, head to toe. Another two seconds. Time trickles away like grains of sand. Not to worry. We saved the most conclusive moment, the end of the end. That moment is coming. It's coming, it's coming. It's here. I love you. I love you. I love you. Bye now.

She pants as she whispers her last few words in this life.

It feels like the world is ending because of us!

Oh, oh, so what if it does, damn it!

THE MOST BEAUTIFUL COUNTRY
IN THE WORLD

AT THE HIGHEST place in the world was the most beautiful country in the world. The abundant trees emitted a floral-scented breeze and clear water trickled down its waterfalls. The fields always yielded a rich crop. People liked to dance and play. Rain came when rain was needed and sunlight shone when sunlight was needed. You'd never hear loud crying from the town. A child once threw a stone toward a flying eagle, blinding it, and that was the town's news for years. Adults worried that kids were becoming increasingly violent, and the high priest offered prayers of self-repentance to the heavens for not having done his job well enough. Word of this beautiful country was spread high and low by birds, insects, and pollen.

Hearing of this wonderful country, people in neighboring countries trickled in one by one with their families. They built their houses next to the valley, burned the forest down and planted corn in its place. After their first winter there, they sent word to their brothers and relatives back home. This country is a blessing from God. Here, you can eat as much butter made with goat milk as you like, the kind you only get to taste at weddings elsewhere. After that, the relatives and brothers packed up and headed toward the beautiful country one by one. The people who arrived in turn sent letters to their relatives and brothers. The roads were clouded with dust and the snow-covered mountaintop became crowded with the bleached skeletons of people who didn't make it. People kept coming, climbing over death and despair. If the father couldn't make it, the son would follow in his footsteps and continue the trip.

The immigrants who came one after another cut down trees and built houses near the valley. They burned the forest to plant corn. The valley became dirty and fields became contaminated. As the soil was ruined, the climate changed. Floods and draughts never ceased, but people didn't know what to do. Bad harvests continued and riots arose. In the end, the country vanished, with only its story remaining on a stone. The name of this country is Maya.

Maya is gone, but there are still people going to Maya.

A SICKNESS THAT
LEADS TO DEATH

I KNOW OF a pitiful chicken that had to eat its own kind. It didn't do it because it wanted to. Just as people have fed chickens crushed leftover eggshells, people fed chicken meat to this pitiful chicken. Humans gave it feed made with what was left of a plucked, disemboweled, and beheaded chicken that was sold hanging by its two feet. The fate of a chicken that ate the feed was the same as its friend that went before him.

What about sheep and cows, which have longer lives than chickens? There were people that fed sheep and cows the meat and bones left behind by their own kind, their friends the sheep and cows. Among these sheep and cows, there were some cows and sheep that started to show symptoms of madness stemming from a disease that caused holes to form in the brain. People feared they'd catch the disease if they ate such cows and sheep. Hence they indiscriminately slaughtered hundreds of sheep and cows. The sheep and those cows were either burned or buried. The name of this bizarre disease is Mad Cow Disease (Bovine Spongiform Encephalopathy), and the name of the disease that people were so afraid of catching is the Creutzfeldt-Jakob Disease (CJD).

I know a story about a snake that ate itself. The snake started eating its tail and worked all the way up to its mouth. As you know, snakes have teeth that point inward, which means they're unable to stop eating what they've begun to eat.

What about people's teeth? What about the so-called notion of development? We should've thought it through before we crawled into our own throats.

THE TV CHEF

LET'S TALK ABOUT noodles today. Oh, as always, I guess we should begin by talking about cooking before getting started with the noodles. Today, I want to introduce you to one of the teachers I'm thankful for. She was a teacher at my high school. She was extremely thin. Still, she ate the same amount as other people. Actually, she might've eaten more, but she still never gained a pound. One year, the class went on a picnic. Do you remember back then how the class president or a kid from a well-off family would bring the teacher's lunch? Well, I guess the kids in her class didn't bring as nice a lunch as the other classes' kids. The teacher was genuinely angry. I mean she wasn't just annoyed or crabby, but explicitly said she was angry. After that incident, she didn't even talk to the kids in her class for three days. Needless to say, from the next picnic on, that teacher's lunch became much fancier. That's right. Just like the dishes we introduce to you on our program. Well, this is The Joy of Cooking! Thank you for joining us, viewers.

It was one summer vacation after that when I ran into this teacher, and her already thin figure was borderline gaunt. I asked her what was going on, and she hesitantly told me that she got sick after eating a dog. What dog? Yes, our family dog, Bokshil. Oh my goodness, you ate your dog? How? Well, I went to the rooftop and called to her. Bokshil, Bokshil. And Bokshil came prancing toward me. So I aimed for the head with an ice axe that I'd hidden behind my back, but missed and wastefully ripped an ear. Terror-stricken, Bokshil scampered away. Then what happened? I lovingly called to her again, Bokshil, come here, good doggy. I think the rascal had doubts about me. She looked at me this way and that way for a long time. But of course, it's a dog, and dogs will always be loyal to their owner. With my axe, I swung at the dog, which came wagging her tail, but this time I hit the edge of her right ear. She bled but didn't die. So I called to her again, but she wouldn't come to me. I called to her for half an hour, until she crawled toward me with her last ounce of faith, tail wagging behind her. I didn't use my axe that time. I realized it'd be difficult to catch the dog with an axe. I grabbed her collar, tied it to a rope, and kicked her over the ledge. I could feel the trembling through the rope in my hand. I looked up at the sky. I felt sorry for her. Still, what could I do? I was hungry. So what'd you do? I wrapped it up in a newspaper, scorched it over a fire and ate it. But I think it made me sick, and I got the runs for three straight days and ended up looking like this. What a waste. That's what my teacher was like. Yup.

Well, what we're making today are noodles with garlic chives. Noodles . . . Do you like noodles? I love them, too. However, I do find it's hard to make dishes that many people love and enjoy well enough for everyone to find delicious. My assistant! Thank you for waiting. Bring in the ingredients. Well, the noodles my adorable assistant friend has brought, these are Saemmul-brand noodles. Good choice. There may be many companies that produce noodles, but you'll be better off selecting a company brand that has a long history. From their line of products, use Saemmul's thin noodles if at all possible. One of the deciding factors for the taste of noodles is their resilience after they've been taken out of boiling water. They shouldn't be too tough, and can't be too weak because they won't feel cooked. They have to be just right. That's why thin noodles are good.

Next, let's talk about the garlic chives. These are noodles with garlic chives, so the quality of the chives is going to determine the overall flavor. There are Korean chives and Chinese chives. When you're looking at chives at the market, be sure to look at the ends. The ones with the pointy ends are Korean chives. Chinese products are thicker in volume and have more rounded edges. Maybe not for other dishes, but for noodles with garlic chives, you want to use Korean chives.

While we cook the noodles, wait a minute, I think we need more water here. Yes, good. When the water boils over, you should pour in some cold water a little bit at a time. When the noodles are fully cooked, they become transparent. You can tell by lifting one up with a chopstick. Don't take them out before they're transparent. If you overcook them, they'll feel swollen, and if you undercook them, they won't be edible. What I'm saying is, you must take them out as soon as they turn transparent. The chives, let's keep talking about the garlic chives. Season the garlic chives with soy sauce, and lightly cook them in oil. But you all know you can't cook them for too long, right? That's right, it destroys the nutrients. Garlic chives are known to be a very strong invigorant. I'm saying that if you eat your garlic chives, your nights will become blissful. Well, if we're done, let's put things on a plate. Yes, very nice.

Let's make the garnishing soy sauce while the noodles are still cooking. Honestly, the most important factor in the taste of this dish is the garnishing soy sauce. Some chopped leeks, a little bit of minced garlic, red pepper powder, sesame seed oil . . . You can't put in too much or too little. I won't explain to you how to pick your garlic and leeks, since we don't have time for that.

Ah, the soy sauce! I almost forgot. When it comes to soy sauce, the Mongo brand is better than the Saemmul brand. Regardless of the type of food, people don't forget their first taste of that food. In fact, your first tastes of food will be the determining standard for all the food you consume over your lifetime. For instance, let's say there is a new snack on the market. If it's a completely new kind of snack, people who get used to the flavor of that snack will say that it's the only authentic kind, even if a different company produces a snack with the same name. The late starters will have a tremendously difficult time trying to break that preconception. The Mongo brand no longer uses water from the Mongolian's well for its soy sauce. Nonetheless, the standard flavor of soy sauce instilled in people's taste buds is the Mongo brand. This is why no matter how well Saemmul makes their soy sauce, it can't be as good as Mongo.

The noodles look ready. Here we go. We'll rinse them well in cold water. Really use your fingers there to get the floury smell out. Good. That's perfect. The garlic chives are ready and so are the noodles . . . what we're missing is, yes, the anchovy broth. You can't really discuss the flavors of a noodle dish without mentioning its broth. When you're making broth, white-bellied anchovies are better than yellow-bellied ones, and bigger is better than smaller. Where are the best anchovies? The ones that come through the port of Chungsan in the South Sea, you got it. No matter where you catch them in the South Sea, they have to come in through the Chungsan port to taste right. Just like how no matter where a yellow corvina is caught in the West Sea, only the ones that come through Younggwang are considered the best. The reason for this? I'm not sure, but since the old days, there's been an unwritten rule, one that all the fishermen near the Chungsan port are aware of, that says the anchovies brought by fishermen who come to Chungsan are the best. Or if they're not the best, they can't go through Chungsan. This is also related to what I was saying about first flavors. If they say a fish from a certain place is the best, then the best fish come through that port, and since the best ones come through that port, people say that that port's fish is the best.

We're going to use an anchovy broth that I made in advance. This is a broth I made with anchovies sent to us by an actual captain of a boat who's a fan of our program. Use a ladle to put some in a bowl, and carefully place the noodles in it. Top it nicely with some garlic chives, and shall we take our chopsticks now? Chopsticks. Yes, chopsticks are important too, but . . . Are you ready? Oh, no rush. Everything we make here, we'll give to you.

Here's today's key point. Flavor is all about that continuous feeling that the dish is special, that it definitely has different qualities than other food. The noodles, garlic chives, soy sauce, and anchovies we used today are all very special. Good-bye everyone, and bon appetit.

THE ULTIMATE LEVEL

MY LORD, YOU were the first person to point out that the gramophone in my house was from the high government office in Hanseong, our capital, which is mostly frequented by the high officials of the top administrative office, Euijeongbu. As you know, my wife gave it to me as a wedding gift and we'd used it for over a decade without any problem. My lord, you said it was deplorable how the gramophone was aged and broken, and couldn't produce quality sound, and you recommended the assembled record players that were brought in, in great quantities, on the ships of Westerners. You praised the assembled record player for having separate compartments which each emitted sound, produced sound, and amplified sound, which allowed you to change the mode in many ways. After what you said, I gave my gramophone away to a scrap collector, but I can't help regretting my rash decision.

Since I did decide to procure a new one, I thought about it and thought some more. Naturally, quality sound comes from a quality product, so if I were to connect the top quality stereo made with empress tree wood from the governmental office with a player from the far away country of France, a loudspeaker from the land of Germany, and a rope from the great land of Russia, it'll have to produce great sound. I've written you, my lord, a letter with the list of items I've obtained over the years, sometimes while struggling, out of breath, and sometimes while being pushed over by the wind into the muddy ground, and had asked you to come visit to hear the sounds. Do you remember what you said then?

"This sound isn't it. That isn't the sound, either. That sound back then was, of course, not right. No matter how well its name is known, how expensive it is, there are considerations to be made for the country of the people who make it, the climate, the level of technology and distribution, the other products produced in that country, the material used in housing, and the intensity of labor. Adding to that, the sound must be adjusted to the listener and also to what's being played, but even if it's adjusted, at best it'll probably be average. If a quality product can become a cheap, low-quality product, and a dog's bowl can become a manger, what good is a product's unique, characteristic sound?"

Then, like a person tumbling down to the bottom of a cliff as the rotten root he's been clutching onto tears away, with the turbulence of a pumpkin rolling down from its place on a roof top, I threw away the dog bowls, which were so-called quality products, and started to buy boards that were blank as white paper, until my floor nearly collapsed from their weight. I could tell my wife was secretly happy thinking I was perhaps doing away with the idleness of being a scholar to open up an electric shop, which would be far more useful to our neighbors, to people in general, to our household. But I had no intention of fulfilling such foolish expectations. Only after spending several years attaching, detaching, discarding, retaining, throwing, and catching well-known tubes, obscure tubes, recognized ropes, newly-made ropes, quiet soundboards and soundboards that jolt your fingertips with a buzz, was I able to hear the sound that made my heart content. And that was when I stammeringly wrote down my delight and surging emotions in a letter to you, my Lord. When you received that letter, you practically ran to my house barefoot. You thoughtfully listened to a melodic recital of a poem by an elderly master of renown who was popular among the party halls or marketplaces hundreds of years ago, played by my gramophone, and you nodded in approval. When you finally spoke, you didn't even notice you were spraying in my face out of enthusiasm.

"I don't have to see how you must have poured your heart into producing such a sound. Listening to it, I can see that you've already placed yourself in a league of your own. Anyway, listen, have you heard the rumors going around in the small towns? Ulgo and Malgo are coming from the West."

My heart sank. In any list I'd laid eyes on over the years, I didn't remember a brand or manufacturer having a name like that. If there indeed were such eccentric-sounding devices in existence, they'd surely have to be above the average, and if they were coming it'd be quite an event. I tried to hide my desperation as I asked you just what kind of systems these were.

You said that Ulgo was being carried over the largest ocean in the world, the Atlantic, and described it as being as small as a fingernail, with small lines protruding from its sides and three lines drawn across its main frame. It cost two nyangs and three pennies. Malgo was to be imported over the world's deepest ocean, the Pacific, and you said it was as big as a pig's toenail, with two lines coming out of each side, one about three centimeters long, and the other about six centimeters long. The Malgo had four lines drawn across its main frame. Its cost: three nyangs. The two names sounded similar, were they made by the same person or made in the same town, or are they maybe part of the same series? Oh, you said that wasn't it. What was known about the Ulgo and Malgo was that they were both small devices that go into the stereo and that they're installed and removed with a tool the size of a toothpick. Twenty were needed for one stereo, and once these devices were installed, they produced a sound so incredible that even the ears of a deaf person would open. You added that trying to find out more about them would be futile, hopeless, even impossible. I sat in a daze listening to you for quite a while, but in truth, my body felt drained and my mind was in disarray. "At least we can be thankful that the Ulgo and Malgo aren't too expensive, so your family won't have to cut and sell their hair again," you said as you walked out my gate, your coat tails fluttering behind you.

For three or four months following that, I locked myself in at home and wandered the tiny maze inside the stereo. At times, I fell to the ground clutching my growling stomach, and at times I swept some dust into my mouth and hastened myself to continue on the dark road. I blamed myself, and sound itself, pulled out my hair in despair, and my sleeves became worn with tears. I can't relay all of the adversities and distress I've endured. When I finally put everything in order and the Ulgo and Malgo arrived, the whole house was in a frenzy. I finally ripped out the old-fashioned components and threw them over the fence, and frantically attached the Ulgo and Malgo using a soldering iron. Even the cat and mouse chasing and running away from each other stopped in their tracks. Can you imagine the delirium of joy when sound echoed out of the sound box? Did you not see the movements of pure insanity? It was a truly exquisite sound that could open the mouth of a mute or a ghost. As soft as a willow, as tickling as the feathers on a duck's breast, and as delicate as a strand of silk. As sonorous as the holler of a centurian or even a chiliarch, as light as a dragonfly grazing the waters of a stream, as translucent as its wings, as magnificent as a snowstorm, the sounds brought out tears and laughter in me. Even you tapped your chest, roaring with laughter, and as you slapped your knees you said this is, beyond doubt, the supreme level of sound. "This was it," you said.

Yet what'd you say to me not even months after that happened? Did you say that it was unbelievable that there is another level, actually a level above any other level, a level that shouldn't even be called a level? You said that those who have the fate to be allowed into the level will do so with only dozens of years of trying, but those not fated to do so won't be allowed onto that level, even if they tried for tens of thousands of years. You said there were fewer than five people in the history of this world who've entered that level and reached nirvana. Why is it that the name of this state of final enlightenment, that level that should not be even called a level seems so trivial and foolish?

"There is an ultimate state one must achieve in soldering. Whether it's a quality product or a dog's bowl, it requires soldering for it to function properly. However, if you keep the iron on for too long, the lead will go on too thick, which will block the flow of energy. If you take it off too soon, the lead will go on thin and won't attach as well. You must keep the iron on for just the right amount of time and take it off with an appropriate amount of movement. However what determines whether one is at an ultimate state of mastery depends on how beautiful the shape of the lead is after the soldering is finished, and whether it has a beautiful shape that is harmonious with the interior of the sound box without being noticeable. When it is noticeable it should touch the heart of the beholder."

Why do I find myself in this state, my lord? I dare ask you, which comes first? Is it the elderly master or the melodic recital of poetry? Is it the gramophone or the sound? Is it the ultimate state or knowing that such an ultimate state exists?

SHAVING ONE'S OWN HEAD

IN ALL OF the temples of the Silla Kingdom, every monk was required to shave their head each morning. It was a daily shaving, so one razor blade was enough. Thanks to all the monks shaving their heads before morning breakfast service, the waters of the Yookdoha River, by which countless temples stood, were always a shade of grey.

If a monk was new at the ritual, an older monk would shave his or her head. Once a person was able to shave his own head he was recognized and accepted as a true monk. Some monks would volunteer to shave the heads of monks who'd lost their limbs during their plight. Shaving another's head meant that you were taking on the other person's plight, so the rule became "A monk is only allowed to shave another monk's hair if that monk is unable to do it himself." That was a commandment that couldn't be breached, like the golden stupa in the headquarters of all temples in the Kingdom of Silla.

Then one year, Prince Moonju entered the Buddhist priesthood. In celebration of this, the king sent him off with a herd of elephants, two hundred male and female servants, gold, amber, agate, pearls, ambergris, and hundreds of sacks of pepper. Monks lined up and filled the road, stretched out for hundreds of kilometers, and welcomed the prince's entourage to the headquarters of all of the country's temples, where there was held the ceremony of shaving Moonju's hair. After the ceremony, there was a reception of tea and refreshments. Moonju, with a shiny, bald head for the first time in his life, asked the question that was on his mind.

"What's going on? It is the golden rule for a monk to shave his own head regardless of whether one's father is the king or one's mother is the queen. If a monk is unable to shave his own head, shouldn't that person leave religious asceticism? I've heard that a designated monk will shave his head instead, isn't this strange to you?'

An elderly monk, who wore a robe made with the feathers of a raven, stood up and replied in a huff, "I am the one you speak of, a monk who shaves the heads of others. You're too green to be asking such questions."

Moonju replied, "What do you do about your own head?"

"I shave my hair with my own hands and feed the waters of the Yookdoha River."

Moonju burst into laughter.

"You're only allowed to shave another person's head in the case that the person is unable to do so himself. You're not allowed to shave the head of a person who's able to do so himself. You're able to shave your head with your own hands. Why is it that you are going against your duty and shaving your own head? Who are you to do so?"

Flushed, the elderly monk was unable to answer this question. The crowd held their heads low and slowly dispersed, blowing on their hands that were covered by their robes, to keep them warm. That's when the saying, "A monk can't shave his own head" came to be. Because of the fault of laughing at another's fault, Moonju ended up becoming a petty ghost of logic, going back and forth between the vast universe and hell for those who committed sins of the tongue.

THE MOST TRAGIC SNOWMAN
IN THE WORLD

THE INUITS (A word in their native language meaning human. Eskimo means "eaters of raw meat" and is a term invented by outsiders) of Quebec love beavers. The fur, which is shiny and insulating, is as valued as cash, and the fatty meat is the most preferred kind for the Inuits living through the long winters of Quebec. However, catching a beaver is a challenging task. Beavers are clever and sensitive animals. A beaver will rarely travel in paths it's not used to. It'll immediately recognize any change in its environment. This is why Inuits devote their lives to becoming excellent beaver hunters.

The saddest thing in this world is that when a hunter has learned everything he can about beavers, he's too old to hunt. Even the god of hunting who leads prey to hunters has no way of helping an Inuit in this situation, and the god of animals who facilitates the catching of animals can do no good.

Hence the elderly Inuit, a snowman that stands with clenched fists, facing the forest, surrounded by an illuminated darkness.

TO MY SECRET WIFE
In Place of the Preface (序), Epilogue (跋), Postscript (後記), Summary (解題), and Discord (異論)

TO WRITE SOMETHING myself, read it myself, and laugh at it myself, is a silly thing to do. Yet because I find it amusing, I every so often read what I've written. I get immersed in it as I read. Who wrote such a commendable novel, allowing me to get a glimpse of truth? It's me. It's the man who doesn't have any idea why or how he wrote that novel. It's the man whose memory is so terrible that, forgetting that he'd written it, says, "what a funny guy, this dude took what I was planning on writing," and grinds his teeth in jealousy.

I think even the people who know me well in these ways are at a loss for words at times. What? You find your own writing funny? You know what, just stay on your high horse. Those are the things they say. So what? I like it, so be it! I attempt to add to this by mumbling to myself, that inside me there is a writer, a reader, and an enjoyer together, and that those three existences are freakishly strange because, clearly divided and distinguished as they are, like a slice of watermelon, they were originally one and the same. My friend who has an imagination that's about three times more powerful than mine, and wit that's about twenty times quicker than mine, immediately jeered at me saying, "You mean you're like a die?"

I've babbled about this to my friends countless times, but I'd like to babble about it one more time today. First, "You have to get into the spirit to get others into the spirit." Second, "You must shudder first to make others fear you." The first describes a shaman, and the second describes a thug who has a knack for breaking glass bottles. For a writer, it'd be, "Have fun writing it and others will have fun reading it," but I'm the kind of person who just can't stand things that aren't fun. (They say that you have to learn how to stand those things to become a master at your art. I don't like masters. I like virtuosos.) The first of the reasons I continue to write novels is that if things are what they are, at least I should be allowed to have some fun. Whether it's fun for others comes later. So what's fun? I'm not telling you.

The issue that follows on the heels of fun is sorrow. One of my high school teachers taught me about the brothers "come," which are the Chinese idioms, "after fun comes sorrow" and "after bitterness comes sweetness." Between the two, I had kept the saying, "after fun comes sorrow" close to my heart. During class, I was punished for laughing and talking about something unrelated to class with my friend sitting next to me. I was made to open fire on Wonsan (a punishment where the punished is made to put his forehead to the ground and lift his butt high up with his arms behind his back). These are the lessons that my teacher told me when I was sweating away like a pig and burning a massive amount of calories. He gave us a set of lessons which were that sorrow finds you after the joy is gone, sorrow where there is still trace of joy is not authentic sorrow, and when pleasure reaches its climax it is the sentiment of sorrow that will seep in. Perhaps it's because the lesson was drilled into me then so rigorously, but even now when I am joyful, I find myself feeling apprehensive about handling the sorrow that will ensue.

What comes after sorrow? We'll talk about that at another opportunity. If that opportunity never comes, then too bad.

I once listened to a song that had the main message, "there are too many me's inside of me," and thanks to my dull hearing, I heard it in several different ways. "There are too many me's inside of thee," "There are too many thee's inside of me," or whatever the original lyrics actually were. I remember thinking that depending on which version you chose it to be, the song would convey a completely different meaning. "There are too many me's inside of me," makes me think of a young person in his early twenties with an autistic tendency. "There are too many me's inside of thee" makes me think of a fortuneteller who deludes the world and deceives people. "There are too many thee's inside of me" just sounds sexual.

There are more than two me's inside of me, but I hope for those two me's that they have less than two them's. I hope for those two them's inside of the two me's to have less than two of them's inside of them, too. That way, at least they will have a normal life. But the best I can do is hope, there's not much I can do about the me inside of me. Especially the me that is sometimes referred to as you.

For that reason, I question whether I really wrote what has my name on it, or whether someone else is writing under my name (or ID). Like a secret snail wife, when nobody's home, she comes out from her water jar and leaves ten, twenty pages worth of writing before hiding herself away again . . . There's something I'd like to ask that secret snail wife when I meet her. Why me? Do I look easy to you? Have you even thought about what my life is like, my snail? Do you like escargot, my wife? Should we take a trip to Siberia to catch ourselves a bear?

Song Sokze was born in 1960, in Sangju, and studied law at Yonsei University. After debuting with the publication of "A Man Wiping the Window" in Literature and Thought in 1986, he began writing fiction in 1994, with his collection of short stories, *Where Bewilderment Lives*. He received the Lee Hyo-seok Literary Award, the Korea Times Literary Award, the Dongseo Literary Award, and the Dongin Literary Award. He also received the Ch'ae Man-sik Literary Award in 2015 for his novel, *The Invisible Man*.

Se-un Kim is a freelance interpreter and translator specializing in literary translation, and was the recipient of a grant from the Literature Translation Institute of Korea. She has been translating for over fifteen years and currently lives in Seoul.